The Fundamentals

and

漢英翻譯
基礎與策略

李孚聲 著

Strategies of

Chinese-to-English

Translation

 崧燁文化

前　言

　　國際間交往的加強似乎應該使不同語言和文化趨於大同，電腦和網絡的普及也似乎應該使翻譯活動趨於簡單，但是，實際情況卻恰恰相反，翻譯活動更加頻繁，內容日益豐富，形式日趨多樣，範圍也越加廣大，翻譯已成為日趨完善的系統工程。這說明，千百年來形成的語言和文化差異還要在相當長的時期中存在下去，翻譯作為一門學問、一種技能、一項職業也會長期存在下去。

　　《漢英翻譯基礎與策略》，顧名思義，就是要對如何有效地進行漢英翻譯做一番較為細緻的探討。本書的重點不在理論，而在實踐。因為實踐是翻譯之本，是翻譯的出發點和歸宿，是翻譯理論的基礎。從事翻譯最忌空談理論，況且，目前翻譯理論非常龐雜，學派林立，這就更不能機械地套用某種翻譯理論了。不套用理論並不是說翻譯沒有理論，要搞好翻譯工作是必須具備系統、紮實的基礎知識和靈活多樣的翻譯策略的。因為在翻譯過程中，"一國文字和另一國文字之間不會沒有距離，譯者的理解和文風跟原作品的內容和形式之間不會沒有距離，而且譯者的體會和他自己的表達能力之間還時常有距離。從一種文字出發，積寸累尺地渡越那許多距離，安穩到達另一種文字里，這是很艱辛的歷程。"（錢鍾書：《林紓的翻譯》）

　　漢英翻譯歷程比英漢翻譯更為艱辛。英漢翻譯可比作從外地回家，又是輕車熟路，譯者心里沒有負擔，因為漢語畢竟是母語，我們對漢語語法、詞匯、語體非常熟悉，一旦理解了英語原文，用母語復述原文內容，並非難事。而漢英翻譯就像離家外出，即便目的地不太陌生，也並非久居之家，譯者心里或多或少總有忐忑。因為英語是外語，即便是學了多年，也變不成母語，其中不知道的東西比比皆是。所以在漢英翻譯中，我們要付出更艱辛的努力，進行更全面的研究。

　　那麼，要想做好漢英翻譯最需要具備什麼能力呢？當然是英文寫作能力，要想把漢語譯成英文，首先要會寫英文。也就是說，先要寫好，才能譯好。要翻譯小說，必須先會寫小說；要翻譯論文，必須先會寫論文；要翻譯詩歌，必須先會寫詩歌。思果先生說得更透徹："不在英文寫作上下苦功，而做中文英譯的工作，是永遠做不好的。不管寫哪種英文，總要像那種英文；如果寫不出那種英文，乾脆不要譯。"

會寫英文了是否就自然而然地會做漢英翻譯了呢？也不一定。翻譯不同於創作，從某種意義上講，更難於創作。在創作時，作者可以自由發揮自己的語言資源，可以揚長避短。而翻譯時，譯者便沒了這種自由。首先，所譯內容不是自己的，選詞造句都要受漢語原文制約。再者，我們的假想讀者是不懂漢語的以英語為母語的人，我們在翻譯時必須時時從他們的語言習慣和文化視角審視我們的譯文，遇到困難和矛盾又無法回避，所以譯者都常常有“為譯好一字而絞盡腦汁”的感覺。因此，要想做好漢英翻譯還需要具備一些語言學方面的基礎知識。一個譯者必須了解翻譯到底是什麼技能，什麼叫做好的譯文，翻譯的原則是什麼，漢英兩種語言到底有哪些差異，翻譯過程都包括哪些環節等。這些問題都要在本書的第一部分論述。

　　對於翻譯策略或技巧的掌握，首先體現在句子層面的翻譯上。英語的單句可以說是翻譯最基本的“單位”或意義層次，翻譯必須從英語的句型構建開始，而不是從漢語句子開始。漢語的“基本單位”或意群可以是一組“流水句”，而英語句子卻是基本固定不變的“主語—謂語—賓語”的模式，漢英翻譯其實就是根據這個模式用英語組句，整個過程可簡化為：

　　找主語→確定謂語→確定次要動詞→判斷語氣→決定語態→選用名詞

　　篇章翻譯是翻譯的最高層次，一個篇章可以是一個段落，也可以是整篇文章。譯文的整體審視要在這個層面進行。譯文的風格、體裁以及詞匯的潤色和檢審，都要在這里完成。

　　本書就是按照“基礎知識→句子翻譯→篇章翻譯”的框架編排的。在翻譯實踐中這的確是段艱辛的歷程，然而，翻譯完成之時帶給譯者的喜悅也是無與倫比的，這種喜悅可以比作經過跋涉攀緣到達山頂的感覺。

　　我們常說漢英翻譯是一種再創造，是指用地道的英語充分表達中文原作“盡在不言中”的含義的整個過程。當你經過艱辛的努力，終於找到了恰當的詞匯、通順的句型、暢達的篇章結構時，你會感到無比的快樂，這種快樂不但不亞於創作，反而更勝於創作。這也許就是翻譯工作的魅力所在吧。

李孚聲

目　錄
CONTENTS

第一部分　基礎知識

第一章　翻譯的實質:科學與藝術　/ 2
一、翻譯的科學性　/ 2
二、翻譯的藝術性　/ 4

第二章　翻譯的原則:信、達、雅　/ 11
一、信（faithfulness）　/ 12
二、達（smoothness）　/ 14
三、雅（elegance）　/ 17

第三章　漢英語言比較:形合與意合　/ 21
一、英譯漢中的障礙　/ 23
二、漢譯英中的障礙　/ 25

第四章　結構轉換　/ 29
一、英譯漢中的結構轉換　/ 32
二、漢譯英中的結構轉換　/ 35

第五章　直譯與意譯　/ 41
一、直譯和意譯的必要性　/ 41
二、異化與歸化的目的性　/ 44

第二部分　句子翻譯

第六章　主語的確定 / 50

一、補充主語 / 51

二、變換主語 / 52

三、識別隱形主語 / 53

四、改從句為主語 / 54

五、以重要信息為主語 / 55

六、採用形式主語 / 56

第七章　連動式的處理 / 57

一、使用介詞 / 58

二、使用分詞 / 60

第八章　從屬信息的翻譯 / 63

一、同位語（appositive） / 65

二、介詞（preposition）與分詞（participle） / 66

三、定語從句（attributive clause） / 67

四、獨立結構（absolute structure） / 70

第九章　虛擬語氣的翻譯 / 72

一、would 的功能和用法 / 73

二、would 與 will 的用法和區別 / 76

三、should 的功能和用法 / 77

四、should 與 must 的用法和區別 / 80

第十章　靜態和動態的翻譯 / 82

一、英語中表示施事者的名詞（doer） / 84

二、英語中表達動態的形容詞（verbal adjective） / 85

三、英語中表示靜態的介詞和介詞短語（prepositional phrase） / 86

第十一章　被動語態的翻譯 / 89

一、與英語相近的"被"字和"為⋯⋯所"結構 / 89

二、其他常用的被動式標記　/ 90

三、表示被動意義的主動式　/ 92

四、表示被動意義的無主句　/ 93

五、通稱或泛稱的運用　/ 94

六、漢語和英語中自身帶有被動意義的詞　/ 96

第十二章　名詞的翻譯　/ 97

一、單數與復數　/ 97

二、特指與泛指　/ 103

第十三章　選詞的技巧　/ 109

一、文本語境（verbal context）　/ 109

二、交際場合語境（physical context）　/ 116

三、歷史語境（historical context）　/ 116

四、文化語境（cultural context）　/ 117

五、慣用語匯（stock expressions）的選擇　/ 118

第三部分　篇章翻譯

第十四章　篇章翻譯的基本步驟　/ 122

例文一　《武訓傳》劇情介紹　/ 122

例文二　溫哥華的居民　/ 126

例文三　我的母親　/ 129

第十五章　原文中文字的合理刪減　/ 134

一、刪減套話　/ 134

例文一　未來廣播電視的發展與管理系統　/ 135

例文二　女性獨身現象　/ 136

二、縮減中式表達方式　/ 137

例文三　農民收藏家　/ 137

三、刪減重複　/ 139

例文四　拒絕　/ 140

第十六章　釋義性翻譯　/ 144

例文一　北京站　/ 145

例文二　我的祖母　/ 147

例文三　兩人世界　/ 148

例文四　中國孩子太辛苦　/ 151

例文五　那晚睡不著　/ 153

第十七章　譯文的綜合潤色和檢審　/ 158

例文一　圖書館　/ 158

例文二　可憐的花　/ 162

例文三　華羅庚的求學之路　/ 165

例文四　紅旗牌轎車　/ 168

例文五　劍橋的鐘聲為她響起　/ 171

第一部分 基礎知識

第一章　翻譯的實質:科學與藝術

第二章　翻譯的原則:信、達、雅

第三章　漢英語言比較:形合與意合

第四章　結構轉換

第五章　直譯與意譯

第一章　翻譯的實質:科學與藝術

翻譯究竟是一門什麼性質的學問？自從有了翻譯以來，人們就在不斷地尋找答案。現在人們終於在總體概念上達成了共識:翻譯是一種跨文化的交際活動，是一門科學，一門藝術，一套技巧，並且有系統的"翻譯理論"。自從人類有了語言、有了交際的願望，翻譯就自然而然地成為操不同語言的人溝通思想、傳遞信息、交流感情的橋梁。對翻譯是一種跨文化的交際活動這一論點，美國翻譯理論家尤金·奈達做出了簡單明了的論述:

翻譯就是用譯文語言自然地復述出與原文最接近的對等信息——首先就語義而言，其次就其風格而言。

Translating consists in reproducing in the receptor language the ***closest natural equivalent*** of the source language message, first in terms of meaning, and second in terms of style (Nida, 1969: 12).

對這個問題，英國翻譯理論家彼得·紐馬克又補充了一點:

翻譯就是按照原作者的意圖把一個文本的意思用另一種語言表達出來。

It is rendering the meaning of a text into another language in the way that the author ***intended the text*** (Newmark, 1988: 5).

這兩個定義涵蓋了翻譯的主要特點:①翻譯的內容（信息 message，原作者的意圖 the author's intention）;②對譯文的要求（最接近原文 closest，表述自然 natural）。

一、翻譯的科學性

毋庸置疑，**翻譯的過程從來就有很強的科學性，有其自身的規律，有其不同於別的學科的系統理論。學習翻譯也有一套有條有理、循序漸進的實施程序。**

其實,翻譯的規律是早已被翻譯家和翻譯工作者有意識或無意識地長期遵循著的實施過程,即理解原文——結構轉換——通順表達。實踐證明,遵守了這個規律,翻譯工作就順利、就有成效;違背甚至偏離了這個規律,翻譯工作就不順利,甚至寸步難行。

先說理解,理解原文是整個翻譯過程的第一步。沒有正確的理解,翻譯出來的內容就不是原作者所要表達的意思,因此整個翻譯活動就從根本上失去了意義。例如:

例 1: Let's *compare notes.*

〔誤〕咱們核對一下筆記吧。　　　　〔正〕咱們**交換一下意見**吧。

例 2: He is a man *dear to* all.

〔誤〕他是見了誰都很親的人。　　　〔正〕大家都**很喜歡**他。

例 3: He has a *weakness* for novels.

〔誤〕他在看小說方面有個弱點。　　〔正〕他**很愛看小說**。

【分析】以上這三個例子說明,如果譯者沒有理解原文中 compare notes, dear to, weakness 的意思,就會出現誤譯。在漢譯英方面也存在對漢語原文的理解問題,例如:

例 4: 他請假坐飛機**回家探親**去了。

〔誤〕He *asked for leave* to go home by air to *see his relatives.*

〔正〕He *is absent on leave* because he left for home by air *for a family reunion.*

【分析】原文中的"了"字已經說明"他已經走了",可是,asked for leave 仍然停留在"請假"的環節上,讀者不知批准了沒有。漢語中的"探親"不能理解為"探望親戚"(to see one's relatives),而是"與家人團聚"(for a family reunion)。

例 5: 我有個朋友今年快四十了,可**個人問題**還沒解決。

〔誤〕I have a friend who is almost 40, but still *hasn't solved his personal problem.*

〔正〕One of my friends is almost 40, but is *still single.*

【分析】原文中的"個人問題"是過去人們經常在口語中暗指的大齡男女的"婚姻大事",譯成 personal problem 就會讓譯文讀者不知所雲。

理解了原文並不意味著就能把意思翻譯出來了,我們必須進行翻譯過程的第二個環節——結構轉換。結構轉換就是打破原語的語法結構,按照譯語的語法結構"破句重組",按照譯文讀者的語言習慣,重新遣詞造句,通順地表達原文作者所要表達的意思或情感。請看下面的範例:

生而瞽者不知有明闇之珠,長處寒者不知寒,久處富者不欣富,無所異則即境相忘也。

(嚴復《天演論》批語)

Without comparison one becomes oblivious to the characteristics of a situation in which he finds himself: a man born blind does not know that a pearl may be gleaming or lusterless, a man used to cold weather taking it for granted, a man in possession of wealth ceases to marvel at affluence.

(王文炯　譯,1992)

在漢語原文中,作者先舉例,結論置末。這和英語語言習慣相左:一般講,英文首先要交代主要成分,重要的事先說,次要的事後說。翻譯的這一規律或原則,對資深翻譯家來說是不言自明的道理,但是對初學者來說卻是必須有條理、分階段地進行學習。結構轉換和通順表達這兩個問題將在後面的章節中詳細論述。

二、翻譯的藝術性

如果說科學講求的是"真",那麼藝術講求的就是"美";翻譯科學研究的結果是"對與錯"的問題,那麼經過藝術創造的譯文就有一個"雅與俗"的問題。

許淵衝在他《翻譯的藝術》一書中說:

忠實於原文內容,通順的譯文形式,發揮譯文的優勢,可以當作文學翻譯的標準。翻譯可以不發揮譯文語言的優勢,但發揮了譯文語言優勢的翻譯卻是更好的翻譯。是否符合必要條件是個對錯問題,是否符合充分條件卻是個好壞問題。

"發揮譯文語言優勢"是評判譯文藝術性的必要條件。好的譯文無論是文學著作,還是政論文章;無論是散文詩歌,還是科普常識,都應該是譯文讀者喜聞樂見的東西,都應該給譯文讀者以美的享受,而不應該讓讀者在讀了我們的譯文之後仍有疑問或不解之處。在這里有必要援引美國作家 Elwyn B. White 對寫作的一段論述:

Economical writing is efficient and aesthetically satisfying. While it makes a minimum demand on the energy and patience of readers, it returns to them a maximum of sharply compressed meaning. You should accept this as your basic responsibility as a writer: that you inflict no unnecessary words on your readers—just as a dentist inflicts no unnecessary pain, a lawyer no unnecessary risk. Economical writing avoids strain and at the same time promotes pleasure by producing a sense of form and right proportion, a sense of words that fit the ideas that they embody—with not a line of "deadwood" to dull the reader's attention, not an extra, useless phrase to clog the free flow of ideas, one following swiftly and clearly upon another.

(李觀儀)

這段話說的是寫作,對翻譯也同樣適用。讀好的譯文,應該像觀賞藝術品一樣,是一種享受。譯文讀者不應該有任何心理負擔,一個有責任心的譯者沒有權力要求讀者做出什麼努力才能看懂譯文。

那麼,漢英兩種語言的優勢何在？又美在哪里？下面分別對此進行分析。

先說漢語,"**現代漢語之美,美在古樸典雅,美在簡潔莊重。此美多源於對傳統的承傳,或曰文言也。**"

(毛榮貴)

請看下列譯例:

例1:

Some kinds of plastics **can be forced** through machines which separate them into long, thin strings, **called** "fibers", and these fibers **can be made** into cloth.

有些塑料可用機器制成細長的線,稱為"纖維",可織布。

【分析】英語句子必須使用三個被動結構才能使全句上下貫通,邏輯完整。漢語句子則沒有必要用這些關聯成分,句意自明;不用這些語法功能詞,結構更緊湊,更為言簡意賅。

例2:

Tell me and I'll forget; show me and I may remember; but involve me and I'll understand.

A. 告訴我的事情,我會忘記;給我看的東西,我可能會記住;但讓我一起干,我就會理解。

B. **耳聞不如目睹;目睹不如篤行。**

【分析】雖然譯文 A 也能達意,但平鋪直敘,缺少文採,讀後讓人興趣索然。譯文 B 既忠實於原文,又體現了中文的簡潔、典雅之美。

例 3：

Studies serve for delight, for ornament, and for ability. Their chief use for delight is in privateness and retiring; for ornament, is in discourse; and for ability, is in the judgment and disposition.

讀書足以怡情,足以博彩,足以長才。其怡情也,最見於獨處幽居之時;其博彩也,最見於高談闊論之中;其長才也,最見於處世判事之際。

（毛榮貴 譯）

【分析】英語原文已經很簡練了,但仍不如漢語譯文典雅、有文採,其中三個"足以",三個"最見於",不但沒有給人以冗餘之感,反而加強了語氣,強調了人們對"開卷有益"的認識。其中的"怡情""博彩""長才"三詞提高了敘述的書卷氣。

例 4：

虞美人

春花秋月何時了? 往事知多少!
小樓昨夜又東風,故國不堪回首月明中。
雕欄玉砌應猶在,只是朱顏改。
問君能有幾多愁? 恰似一江春水向東流。

The Lost Land Recalled
—Tune "The Beautiful Lady Yu"

When will there be no more autumn moon and spring flowers
For me who had so many memorable hours?
My attic which last night in vernal wind did stand
Reminds me cruelly of the lost moonlit land.

Carved balustrades and marble steps must still be there,
But rosy faces cannot be as fair.
If you ask me how much my sorrow has increased,
Just see the over-brimming river flowing east!

（許淵衝 譯）

【分析】這是南唐後主李煜追憶故國,抒發亡國之痛的絕世之作,充滿了無限愁情。雖然許淵衝的譯作很好地保持了原詞的詞韻,但是漢語原作所給人的那種淒美意境卻無法再現。

另外,大量的雙音節詞和四音節詞的運用使漢語有一種特有的均衡美和節奏美。由於這一傾向的影響,漢語音節勻稱,詞語和句式往往成雙成對,對偶、對照、排比、反覆和重疊成了中國人所喜聞樂見的修辭方式。

例 5:

It was a day as fresh as grass growing up and clouds going over and butterflies coming down can make it. It was a day compounded from silences of bee and flower and ocean and land, which were not silences at all, but motions, stirs, flutters, risings, fallings, each in its own time and matchless rhythm.

綠草萋萋,白雲冉冉,彩蝶翩翩,那日子是如此清新可愛;蜜蜂無言,春花不語,海波聲歇,大地音寂,那日子又是如此靜謐平和。然而,靜並非真靜,世間萬物以其特有的節奏,或動,或搖,或震,或起,或伏。

【分析】原文中的 silences of bee and flower and ocean and land 譯成"蜜蜂無言,春花不語,海波聲歇,大地音寂" 四音節詞,silences 譯為四個不同的詞:"無言"、"不語"、"聲歇"、"音寂",這樣讀起來更為生動,更有詩意,節奏感更強。

在英譯漢時,不用四音節詞或四字成語,只能達到通順的效果,用了這類詞,譯文就有了節奏美,就有了文採。試比較下列詞語的漢譯:

英語原文	普通翻譯	藝術化翻譯
extremely urgent	非常緊急	十萬火急
commit the same error	犯同樣的錯誤	重蹈覆轍
full of conceit	充滿自負	目空一切
miss a good chance	失去一個好機會	與良機失之交臂
fellow sufferers	一道受苦的人	難兄難弟
make a superficial change	只作表面改變	換湯不換藥
very timid	非常膽小	膽小如鼠
very strong	非常強壯	強壯如牛
keep quiet	不吱聲	噤若寒蟬
do evil things openly	公開地干壞事	明火執仗

續表

英語原文	普通翻譯	藝術化翻譯
be full of anxiety and worry	十分掛念，放心不下	牽腸掛肚
very anxious to return home	回家心切	歸心似箭
accelerate the speed	加快速度	快馬加鞭
not cut relations completely	沒有徹底斷絕關係	藕斷絲連
underestimate one's capabilities	低估自己的能力	妄自菲薄

毫無疑問，四字成語的運用提高了譯文的藝術性，使中國人讀起來更感親切。

那麼，英語的藝術美又展現在哪里呢？**英語之美，美在表達精當，敘述準確，條理分明**。請看下列譯例：

例6：

剛來北京那年，真是吃了不少苦頭。還不錯，遇見了一個大好人，就是外語學院的王教授。他可是我真正的好老師啊！沒有他的指點和幫助，我今天還不知道在哪兒呢！

When I first came to Beijing, life wasn't smiling on me, but I *had the good luck* to meet a really good man, Professor Wang of a foreign language institute. He was my teacher *in the true sense of the word.* Without his advice and help, I *wouldn't be* where I am today.

【分析】漢語原句是個無主句，句中的"還不錯"聽起來也非常模糊，什麼叫"還不錯"？怎麼個"不錯"法？英語的 I had the good luck 就清楚多了，講話人遇到王教授是因為"幸運"。在翻譯"他可是我真正的好老師啊！"一句時，無論你用什麼形容詞，如 really, truly, extremely, certainly，都不能譯出講話人的心情。一句慣用語 in the true sense of the word 就解決了問題。"沒有他的指點和幫助，我今天還不知道在哪兒呢！"屬虛擬語氣，中國人一聽便知，但在英譯中，必須用語法手段明確表示出來：I wouldn't be where I am today。

例7：

從我的觀察，他精神一好便什麼都好，出些過錯他反而安慰你，逗你開心。怕就怕他連續幾夜睡不好覺，精神長期高度緊張，那時最容易發脾氣。

As I observe, when he is in a good humor, *he will find everything agreeable,* even mistakes; he will **talk to the offender kindly and playfully so as to make him forget his mistakes.** But it is an entirely different story if he hasn't slept for several nights or when his nerves are on edge. That is when he easily becomes irritable.

【分析】原文里的"他精神一好便什麼都好"一句,意思很模糊,英譯為 when he is in a good humor, he will find everything agreeable,意思就很清楚了:"他精神一好,就覺得事事順心。""出些過錯他反而安慰你,逗你開心。"誰的過錯? 怎麼逗人開心? 英譯文中交代得清清楚楚:he will talk to the offender kindly and playfully so as to make him forget his mistakes.

例8:

在許多北京人的記憶中,四合院是個令人快樂的所在,小院兒里住著幾戶人家,二十幾個人。同院的孩子一起玩兒,一塊兒長,就像一家人。雖然屋子裏沒有暖氣,沒有下水道,又沒有洗手間,生活不太方便,可鄰居們一塊兒住著,出出進進地道聲辛苦,日子過得也挺愉快。

The residential compound with houses around a courtyard, as many Beijingers recall, was a happy kind of place. There were often four to ten families with an average of 20 people sharing the courtyard complex. The children played together and grew up like one family. Inconveniences like the absence of central heating, **indoor toilets** and plumbing might make life somewhat hard, but the dwellers **enjoyed sharing a place that way.** They **felt quite close to each other when they exchanged greetings everyday.**

【分析】原文中的"洗手間""日子過得也挺愉快""出出進進地道聲辛苦"都不甚明確,在英譯文里必須分別用 indoor toilets, the dwellers enjoyed sharing a place that way, They felt quite close to each other when they exchanged greetings everyday 明確地翻譯出來。

例9:

如今,北京的家庭平均人口呈下降趨勢。70 年代家庭平均人口是 4 人,80 年代就變成 3.5 人了。到了 1990 年,人口普查顯示出平均人口是 3.2 人。另外,越來越多的人希望同他們的父母或已婚子女分開來過。老舍筆下的"四世同堂"式的大家庭只能在小說中才能找到了。

Today families in Beijing are getting smaller. In the 70s the average size was four. A decade later it dropped to 3.5. The 1990 city census showed a further shrink to 3.2. **Another reason for smaller families** is that an increasing number of people now live in separate houses from their parents or married children. Big families as "*four generations under one roof*" can only be found *in print.*

【分析】原文中的"另外"的意思不是很明確,所以必須譯成 Another reason for smaller families。這篇短文議論的主題是北京的家庭結構,不必介紹老舍先生,所以在譯文里沒有提及。"'四世同堂'式的大家庭只能在小說中才能找到了"中的"小說"也不準確,所指單一,在回憶錄、報告文學、散文等文體中仍會出現"四世同堂"這一說法,因此譯文用 in print 對之。

總之,翻譯中體現出的藝術性、創造性取決於是否"發揮譯文語言優勢"。成功的譯文在內容達意的基礎上要揚譯文所長,避原文所短,真正達到理想的美學效果。

思考題

1. 如果說翻譯是一門科學,其科學性、規律性體現在哪里?
2. 如果說翻譯是一門藝術,如何發揮其藝術性? 從哪個角度體現譯文的藝術性?

第二章　翻譯的原則:信、達、雅

　　說到翻譯的原則,我們不能不說我國近代啓蒙思想家、翻譯家嚴復(1854—1921)提出的"信、達、雅"之說。從 1898 年嚴復提出此說到 2008 年,"信、達、雅"作為指導翻譯實踐的原則,已有 110 年的歷史。在這麼長的歷史時期中,中國社會發生了天翻地覆的變化,但這個學說仍然具有很強的生命力,仍然為翻譯界所引用,所研究,所發展,這不能不說是個奇跡。按照羅新璋在《我國自成體系的翻譯理論》一文中的觀點,"信、達、雅"之說"之所以屢推不倒,積久而著,只有一個解釋,就是信達雅在相當程度上概括了翻譯工作的主要特點,說出了某些規律性的東西……"這個解釋是非常恰當的。

　　讓人驚嘆的是,嚴復的"信、達、雅"之說與泰特勒(Alexander Fraser Tytler)的三原則和奈達(Eugene Nida)的"動態對等"論,有著異曲同工之妙。現列舉如下:

　　泰特勒的三原則:

　　(1)譯文應完全再現原作的思想觀點。(可謂"信")

　　　　A translation should give a complete transcript of the ideas of the original work.

　　(2)譯文的風格和筆調特點應與原作相同。(可謂"雅")

　　　　The style and manner of writing in a translation should be of the same character with that of the original.

　　(3)譯文應和原作同樣流暢自然。(可謂"達")

　　　　A translation should have all the ease of original composition.

(沈蘇儒,1998:121)

　　奈達的"動態對等"論:

　　翻譯就是用譯文語言自然地復述出與原文最接近的對等信息——首先就語義而言,其次就其風格而言。

　　Translating consists in reproducing in the receptor language the ***closest natural*** *equivalent* of the source language message, first in terms of meaning, and second in terms of style. (Nida, 1969).

　　在這三者中,嚴氏三原則的概括性最強,給後人留下了廣闊的想象空間和發揮餘地。本章就以信、達、雅為脈絡,對翻譯的原則進行分析。

一、信 (faithfulness)

　　從理論上講,"信"指的是**譯文不但要忠實於原作的思想、觀點和內容,還要忠實於原作者的寫作意願和預期目的**。但是,在現實中,這只不過是讀者和譯者的良好願望而已,忠實於原作只是相對而言,能達到奈達所說的"最接近的對等"就很不容易了,雖然要完全把負載著一個民族文化某個側面的語言,原原本本地復制到另一種語言中,是絕對辦不到的事,但我們仍要朝著這個方向努力。為求"信",譯者必須徹底理解原文的意思,並在譯語中找到接點。這在英漢翻譯中體現得最為明顯。請看下列譯例:

例 1：No man can have too many friends.
　　〔誤〕沒人能有太多的朋友。　　　　　　〔正〕朋友越多越好。

例 2：You cannot take sufficient care.
　　〔誤〕你不可能做到足夠小心。　　　　　　〔正〕你要特別小心。

例 3：The importance of this conference cannot be exaggerated.
　　〔誤〕這次大會的重要性是不能被誇大的。　〔正〕這次大會極為重要。

例 4："Mary, you're so pretty today. " ("瑪麗,你今天可真漂亮。")
　　"You're just being polite. "
　　〔誤〕"你真有禮貌。"　　　　　　　　　　〔正〕"你真會說話。"

例 5：I would feel guilty to take such an expensive gift.
　　〔誤〕收這麼貴的禮物我感到內疚。
　　〔正〕這麼貴的禮物我真是愧領了。

例6：I couldn't care less for those meetings.
〔誤〕我不能不重視這些會議。　　　　〔正〕我才不去開那種會呢。

例7：His handwriting is strange to me.
〔誤〕他的筆跡對我來說很奇怪。　　　　〔正〕他寫的字我不認得。

例8：The old man is not at home to anyone except relatives.
〔誤〕只要親戚一來,這個老人準不在家。
〔正〕除了親戚外,老人概不見客。

例9：You are a sight for sore eyes.
〔誤〕你是讓人望眼欲穿的人。　　　　〔正〕你可來了。

例10：He is ignorant to a proverb.
〔誤〕他太無知了,連一個成語都不知道。　〔正〕他的無知是出了名的。

漢英翻譯中不忠實原意的誤譯也比比皆是：

	原文	誤譯	正譯
1	密碼	secret code	password
2	白蟻	white ants	termite
3	休息室	restroom	lounge
4	蝴蝶結	butterfly knot	bow
5	方便面	convenient noodles	instant noodles
6	隱形眼鏡	invisible glasses	contact lenses
7	課堂測驗	classroom test	pop-quiz
8	我的話講完了,耽誤大家時間了。	My speech is over. Sorry to have wasted your time.	Thank you for your attention.
9	飯菜不好,請多包涵。	The dishes are not good. Please excuse me.	Hope you'll like the dishes I've prepared.

以上這些例句中的誤譯只是"忠實於"原文的表面結構,沒有忠實於原文的深層意思,"雖譯猶不譯也"。

二、達（smoothness）

　　"達"的意思是**譯文通順達意**，是對翻譯的基本要求。**譯文要簡明、易懂**，讀起來非常舒服。**絕不能佶屈聱牙、生澀難懂**。以下兩例就是通達的翻譯。

例1：A："How much did you suffer in the war?"
　　　B："***Plenty***"，the old soldier said.
　　　A："戰爭中你吃了多少苦啊?"
　　　B："**一言難盡**"，老兵說。

例2：A："Hyde park you said，didn't you? I'll be there to cheer you."
　　　B："***It's a promise***，"he said.
　　　A："你說是去海德公園，是不是? 我一定去給你捧場。"
　　　B："那就**一言為定**啦，"他說。

　　下面比較一下拙劣翻譯與通順翻譯的區別。

例3：This restaurant used to ***offer slow and rude service***，***less than appetizing food and an appalling toilet***.
　　　〔拙譯〕這家飯館以前總是**提供慢而粗魯的服務、不可口的飯菜和可怕的廁所**。
　　　〔順譯〕這家飯館以前是**上菜慢，服務差，飯菜糟，廁所髒**。

例4：With the reshuffle，the new prime minister has put together ***a much younger cabinet with a broader spread of talent***.
　　　〔拙譯〕經過改組，新當選的總理組成了**一個大大年輕了並含有更多賢能之士的內閣班子**。
　　　〔順譯〕新任總理的內閣班子經過改組，**大為年輕化了，而且更廣泛地吸納各方面的賢能之士**。

例5：Farmers now sell vegetables ***at moving prices determined by their supply and the customers' demand***.
　　　〔拙譯〕現在農民賣菜，價格根據菜的供應量和顧客的需求而浮動。
　　　〔順譯〕現在農民賣菜，價格**隨行就市**。

例 6： The ASEAN Summit Conference in Bangkok was a ***security nightmare*** for Thailand.

〔拙譯〕在曼谷召開的東盟峰會，對泰國來說，簡直是一場**安全噩夢**。

〔順譯〕曼谷東盟峰會的**安全保衛工作**對泰國來說簡直是**一大難題**。

例 7： To explain the plot of a play to this kind of actress is ***a director's nightmare***.

〔拙譯〕給這樣的演員說戲對導演來說就是**噩夢**。

〔順譯〕給這樣的演員說戲，讓導演**大傷腦筋**。

　　從以上拙譯句子不難看出，譯者沒有考慮到漢語讀者的語言習慣，一味按照英語句子結構直譯，結果使人覺得就像在聽粗通漢語的外國人講話一樣，很別扭，根本談不上通順達意。目前在媒體中流行的蹩腳譯例可以說俯拾即是：

原文	蹩腳翻譯	正確譯法
zebra crossing	斑馬線	**人行橫道**
philharmonic orchestra	愛樂樂團	**交響樂團**
The Grapes of Wrath	《憤怒的葡萄》	**《怒火叢焰》/《天怒》**
food security	糧食安全	**溫飽/糧食保障供給**
military presence	軍事存在	**駐軍**
CEO	首席執行官	**執行總裁**
political correctness	站穩政治立場	**使用恰當語言**
action movies	動作片	**武打片**
field survey	野外調查	**實地考察**
humanitarian crises	人道主義危機	**人員傷亡、財產損失**
Formula One	一級方程式	**一號規格車賽**
to make a wish	許願	**求願**
sexual harassment	性騷擾	**調戲**
I can't see you today. It's a bad day.	我不能去看你了，今天是個壞日子。	**今天我實在太忙了**，不能去看你了，改天吧。
Nobody claimed responsibility for the bombing.	沒有人聲稱對爆炸負責。	沒有人聲明稱爆炸是他們**所為**。

續表

原文	蹩腳翻譯	正確譯法
He had barely enough time to catch the train.	他僅有足夠的時間趕上火車。	**他差點兒沒趕上火車。**
The more work we give our brain, the more work they are able to do.	讓腦子工作得越多，它就能干更多的工作。	**腦子越用越好使。**

在漢譯英時，由於母語的干擾，更容易出現拙劣翻譯。例如：

例 8： 柑橘生長在南方，從前在北京賣得價錢很貴。

〔拙譯〕Oranges, *produced* in south China, used to *be sold at very high prices.*

〔順譯〕Oranges, *which grow* in south China, used to *be very expensive.*

例 9： 這時候，影片切入了一個鏡頭，一輛摩托車，上面坐著三個警察，朝橋上衝了過來。

〔拙譯〕At the moment, a scene appears in the movie, in which a motorbike, with three policemen sitting on it, is charging to the bridge.

〔順譯〕The movie cuts to a motorbike with three cops on it racing toward a bridge.

例 10： 這位跳高選手，試跳三次不成，只好空手而歸。

〔拙譯〕Having failed in three *trial jumps*, this high jumper *gave up trying again.*

〔順譯〕Having failed in three *attempts*, this high jumper *had to go home empty-handed.*

例 11： 做生意的要訣是誠信。

〔拙譯〕*Honesty* is the *knack of doing business.*

〔順譯〕*Good faith* is *key to success in business.*

例 12： 這一帶治安情況不好。

〔拙譯〕Public security *situation* in this area is *bad*.

〔順譯〕Public security is *a problem* in this area.

例 13：寫東西的時候，盡量不用你不熟悉的詞語。

〔拙譯〕Don't use the words you are ***not familiar with*** in your writing.

〔順譯〕When writing, avoid using words and phrases ***you don't know much about.***

三、雅（elegance）

"雅"是翻譯的最高境界，百餘年來，翻譯家、學者對此有許多不同的解釋。無論在哪個時期，這個"雅"字都是公認的絕對富含美學價值的褒義詞，常常用在"文雅""高雅""典雅""風雅""雅致"等美好的詞中，因此人們很容易按這些詞的意思形成"雅"的概念。

但是在翻譯領域，"雅"字要在翻譯的藝術性框架內進行審視，必須在譯文達到"信"和"達"的基礎上來理解。能達到"雅"字境界的譯品應該是在**內容上忠實於原作，在表述上通達明快，在文字上正確規範，在文化上符合譯文讀者的語言習慣和審美價值**的作品。請看下列譯例：

例 1：

獅子林

獅子林以假山為主要景色，假山約占全園面積的一半，山上奇峰巨石林立，有"含暉"、"吐月"、"玄玉"、"昂霄"等峰名，"獅子峰"為眾峰之冠。百年古樹盤生於石縫之間，誰見了不認為是真正的山林！山上有石洞二十一，高低盤旋，左右迂回，幽深莫測，宛如迷宮。入洞忽而登上山峰，忽而下到洞底，眼看山窮水盡，卻又豁然開朗；咫尺之間，可望而不可即；明明相向而來，卻是背道而去；看看不遠，走走沒完，必須循規蹈矩，方可順利出洞，真可謂妙趣橫生。每換一洞，景象各異，有"桃源十八景"之說。整個假山，全用太湖石疊成，外表看去，異常雄渾，內部卻玲瓏剔透，處處空靈。這種卓越的技藝，充分反應了古代勞動人民的智慧和藝術創造才能。

真趣亭上掛有匾額，上書"真趣"二字，據說為清朝皇帝乾隆所書。乾隆南遊來蘇州，找了一個有學問的小官黃興祖陪他遊此園，他穿假山、覽廳堂、頗覺有趣。乘興揮筆寫了"真有趣"三字。黃感到俗氣又不敢直言。只好拐彎抹角地說"皇上把中間的'有'字賜給我吧。"於是成了現在的匾額。亭側石舫是中心池的主要觀賞點。這里山光波影，亭橋倒映其間，是丹青妙手駐足的地方。池中的湖心亭和曲橋，使池面有層次，景色更為深遠。

Lion Grove

Artificial hills are the main features of the garden. These hills, which take up almost half of the space of its compound, rise in fantastic shapes and are called by such fancy names as **Radiance** (Hanhui), **Rising Moon** (Tuyue), **Black Jade** (Xuanyu), **Challenging the Sky** (Angxiao), and **Lion Peak** (Shizifeng), which is the most majestic of them all. With ancient trees growing out of the crevices in them, these rock formations look like real hills. On the outside, they are all rugged hills built entirely with Taihu rocks, but inside they are exquisitely hollowed, **demonstrating the imagination of their creators.**

The twenty-one caves in the hills, each offering a different sight from the other, are connected by a maze of tunnels which rise in one place only to drop in another as they wind their way to mysterious destinations. A walk in this maze can be an exciting experience. One may suddenly find himself at the top of these hills, or at the bottom of a cave. What seems to be the dead end of a tunnel may turn out to be the beginning of another path, what looks like a short distance may take a long time to cover, and what appears to be the way leading to where one wishes to go may end in quite the opposite direction. The stroller will invariably lose his way in these caves unless he follows the proper path.

The two words ZHEN QU (true fascination) on the large tablet that hangs in the True Fascination Pavilion are said to have been the work of the Qing emperor Qianlong. When the emperor was visiting the garden, he was fascinated by its artificial hills and buildings. In a rapturous mood, he wrote three words ZHEN YOU QU (It's truly fascinating). A scholarly petty official by the name Huang Xingzu who was accompanying the emperor found the expression vulgar. Afraid to tell the emperor what he thought of the three words, he said diplomatically, "Would Your Majesty be kind enough to make me a gift of the middle word?" and the result is the more elegant ZHEN QU that the tablet shows.

The stone boat next to the True Fascination Pavilion is the chief attraction of the main pond in the garden. The reflections in the pond are so beautiful that they will keep an artist at this place for long hours. The pavilion in the middle of the pond together with its zigzag bridges breaks the otherwise monotonous water surface and lends depth to the surrounding scenery.

（王文炯　譯）

　　譯好這段文字並不容易，因為它用了很多漢語的修辭手法，如中國人在給景點起名時，往往按照景點的地形地貌，以中國人的審美標準為取向，起一些富於寫意特點的、具有朦朧美的名字，譬如文中的"含暉"、"吐月"、"玄玉"、"昂霄"、"獅子峰"等峰名，譯文讀者看到這些景點名稱的英譯（Radiance, Rising Moon, Black Jade, Challenging the Sky, Lion Peak）時，是能夠體會到這個特點的。

　　文中的"充分反應了古代勞動人民的智慧和藝術創造才能"一句，是套話，譯做 demonstrating the imagination of their creators 就很貼切。另外，原文中關於"真趣亭"一段，涉及漢語表達方式的雅俗問題，例如："真有趣"和"真趣"的區別。"真有趣"是一句口語，不應該是題詞，但是作為下級官吏的黃興祖，如果給皇上糾正錯誤，就犯了"輕君之罪"，但又不肯把皇上的題字原封不動地制成匾額，而自己又不能隨便改動，只好用變通的方法（diplomatically）以達到既保留了皇上的題詞，又沒有冒犯君顏的效果。這段趣事的翻譯是相當到位的。

例 2:

文房四寶

　　在中國，筆、墨、紙、硯，就是人們所說的"文房四寶"，在中華文明的傳承中起了重要作用。作為文化藝術工具，文房四寶以其獨特性能催生了漢字特有的書法藝術，也促使中國畫形成了獨特的風格。它們不僅有實用價值，經過用繪畫、書法、雕刻等加以裝飾後，它們本身也成為供人觀賞的藝術品，並逐步成為收藏品。文房四寶品類繁多，豐富多彩，選材制作不斷趨於完善、精美，歷代都有名品、名匠產生，成為一種深厚的文化積澱。

　　在當今時代，使用筆、墨、紙、硯進行學習、寫作的人越來越少了；但是，在中國的書法、美術、收藏以及修身養性活動中，它們仍起著不可替代的作用，仍是中國傳統文化寶庫中絢麗的瑰寶。

Four Treasures of the Study

The four items of Chinese stationery, the writing brush, ink, paper and inkslab, have contributed a great deal to the shaping of Chinese cultural heritage. Chinese calligraphy and painting, for example, owe to them their unique shape and style. In addition to the practical purposes they serve, they themselves are works of art and collectors' items when they are embellished with pictures, carvings and words. Thanks to the craftsmen, many of them masters of the trade, who never stopped enhancing their skills and always looked for better material to make them, there has never been an age in China that passed without the production in large numbers and great variety of works of art of this kind so superb that they have earned a place in the rich legacy of Chinese culture.

Today fewer and fewer people are dependent on the stationery items of this kind for everyday use, but they will remain irreplaceable in our culture for their immense aesthetic value.

（王文炯 譯）

這段漢語原文可以說是邏輯性不太強，又用了不少時髦套話的一段文字，例如：“書法、美術、收藏以及修身養性活動”，這四件事放在一起說是沒有邏輯性的，再說怎樣理解中國的修身養性？這恐怕很難說清楚。“使用筆、墨、紙、硯進行學習、寫作”意指太寬泛，因為在中國練習毛筆字、畫畫都可以看做是學習，但在英語國家練字並不是 learning 或 study，這里譯者譯為 for everyday use 是很恰當的。另外，“在中華文明的傳承中起了重要作用”、“成為一種深厚的文化積澱”和“是中國傳統文化寶庫中絢麗的瑰寶”都是中國常見的套語，非常籠統，但在譯文中卻必須運用有實際含義的詞語表述。這兩句話分別譯做 they have earned a place in the rich **legacy** of Chinese culture 和 they will remain irreplaceable in our culture for their immense **aesthetic value**，是很有創意的。

“雅”是在“信”和“達”的基礎上達到創造性翻譯的最高層次，我們說翻譯是再創造，是指翻譯作為跨語言、跨文化交流的手段，會遇到各式各樣的困難，譯者必須發揮自己的聰明才智，創造性地去克服困難，而不是脫離原文的“潤色加藻”（錢鍾書）。給“雅”下定義，王佐良在《嚴復的用心》一文中說得非常精辟：“嚴復的‘雅’是同他的第一，亦即最重要的一點——‘信’——緊密相連的。換言之，雅不是美化，不是把一篇原來不典雅的文章譯得很典雅，而是指一種努力，要傳達一種比詞、句的簡單的含義更高更精微的東西：原作者的心智特點，原作的精神光澤。”這個定義正是本書在論述翻譯的原則時所依據的理論基礎。

思考題

1. 為什麼說翻譯是一種再創造？
2. 在“信、達、雅”三原則中，哪個原則最能體現譯者的主觀能動性和翻譯風格？

第三章　漢英語言比較：形合與意合

　　翻譯學習始於兩種語言的比較，翻譯理論與技巧是建立在對不同語言和文化的對比分析基礎之上的。我們有時感到翻譯比創作還要紛繁複雜，歸根結底，原因就在於漢英之間的語言差異和文化差異。

　　漢語和英語分屬不同語系，在詞形、詞義、語法範疇、句子結構上存在著很多差別。那麼，哪些差別給翻譯造成的困難最大、最難解決呢？答案恐怕要到兩種語言的本質區別上去找。英語屬形態語言（inflectional language），表達意思離不開詞形變化，離不開明確的語法標識。英語中的大部分語法標識，集中體現在動詞的形態變化上，形成以動詞形態變化為主軸的句法結構模式，意義緊緊與句法形態相結合，注重顯性銜接（overt cohesion），以形顯意。因此英語也可稱為形合語言（hypotaxis），句法結構嚴謹，連接成分必不可少，句群組合環環相扣，嚴密緊湊，表意精確。

　　而漢語是非形態語言（non-inflectional language），這是因為漢語是方塊字和象形文字，語法關係不可能通過字形或詞形變化來表示。漢語的語法意義只能通過詞匯手段，如加詞、減詞或改變詞序來表示，連接成分或有或無。這就使漢語句法結構松散，許多意義不必明說，只讀詞句便可意會，因此被稱作意合語言（parataxis）。

　　"意合與形合之別其實也就是語篇連貫的隱顯的不同。漢語的意合無須借助詞匯語法的銜接手段，僅靠詞語和句子內涵意義的邏輯關係（或靠各種語境和語用因素），便能構成連貫的語篇；英語則往往少不了詞匯語法的顯性銜接，即從語言形式上把詞語句子結合成語篇整體"（何善芬，2002：472）。對此王力做過形象的比喻："西洋語的結構好像**連環**，雖則環與環都聯絡起來，畢竟有聯絡的痕跡；中國語的結構好像**無縫天衣**，只是一塊一塊的硬湊，湊起來還不讓它有痕跡。西洋語法是硬的，沒有彈性的；中國語法是軟的，富於彈性的。"

　　就是在非正式的場合，英語國家的人離了篇章標記（discourse markers）是不能表達思想的。常用的語篇標記可大致分為以下十類：

(1) 時間順序：In the first place / Next / Previously / Secondly / After that / While / Then / Last / When

(2) 強調：The point you must remember is… / I'd like to emphasize… / Let me repeat. / The next point is crucial to my argument.

(3) 解釋：In other words / Let me put it this way / That is to say

(4) 舉例：For example / For instance / Let's take… / An example of this was…

(5) 轉換話題：Changing the subject / Now let's think about (look at, consider, turn our attention to)…

(6) 因果：So / Therefore / Thus / Since / As / Because / Consequently / As a result

(7) 遞進：Moreover / Furthermore / What's more / Also / In addition

(8) 轉折：But / Nevertheless / However / Although / Yet / On the other hand

(9) 假設：If / Unless / Assuming that

(10) 總結：To summarize / To sum up / In conclusion / Briefly then / It amounts to this / As we have seen

這些標記在自然的講話或採訪中是必不可少的。下面是一則實例：一個日化公司生產部經理接受採訪談她的業務發展。

Well, I joined the company as a marketing assistant back in 1997 and my duties *then* (時間順序) were quite different to my present duties as product manager. *Now*, (時間順序) I'm responsible for both our soap range and hair-care products, whereas *before* (對比) I was getting general marketing experience. *For example*, (舉例) I assisted the marketing manager by collecting and analyzing data. *In particular*, (強調) I was involved in market research for our soap products. My responsibilities have changed a lot, of course. *In those days*, (時間順序) I used to be just a member of a team, *but now*, (轉折) I've got five people working under me and I'm completely responsible for the launch of a new range of hair products next year. There's a lot more work. *On the other hand*, (對比) it's much more varied. The actual hours I spend in the office are nearly the same as before. *However*, (遞進) I do tend to take more work home these days. This is something our marketing manager, who is directly above me, thinks quite normal.

　　我們在翻譯中出現的諸多困難幾乎都源自漢英語言的這個差別。英譯漢時，我們總是被一些英語的句子結構、介詞短語所困擾，弄不清其中的確切含義；漢譯英時，我們常常找不到翻譯的"突破口"，不知道哪里是起點。另外，儘管我們知道漢語里"不言自明"的語義，但又苦於找不到英語中相應的對接表達法。因此，**英譯漢時，我們必須先分析句子的結構、形式或固定短語，才能確定句子的功能、意義，至於漢語中的信息排列，要按漢語的習慣；漢譯英時，我們往往要先分析詞彙和句子的整體意義和功能，分清主次，才能確定譯文的句子結構和形式。**下面分別舉例並分析。

一、英譯漢中的障礙

1. 句型差異

　　由於英語靠句型、詞形變化來達意，很多句子在漢語讀者看來顯得較長。而漢語沒有形態變化，詞的先後次序一般是按照時間順序和邏輯關係來排列的。換言之，漢語造句主要採用"流水記事法"（chronicle style），常用分句或流水來逐層敘述思維的各個過程（streamline the thoughts）。造句常常"短小精悍"，英譯漢時常常要破句重組，化繁為簡。請看下列譯例：

例 1： The true American hamburger came into existence in St. Louis, at the Louisiana Purchase Exposition in 1904. *A harried cook* at the fair quickly slapped *broiled* beef patties between buns and served them to *a demanding crowd*, *which* gulped them down joyously.

真正的美國漢堡包是 1904 年在聖路易斯市舉行的一次交易會上產生的。有一天，在交易會的餐廳里一群等著吃飯的人催促著快上菜，急得一個廚師只好飛快地把烤熟的牛肉餅夾在面包里端上來應急，那群餓急了的人立刻痛痛快快地大口吃了起來。這就是最早的美國漢堡包。

【分析】原文段落只有兩句話，但卻講述了美國漢堡包的由來。由於運用了詞形變化和從句，句子結構顯得緊湊、簡潔，所傳達的內容很多。例如：*A harried cook* at the fair quickly slapped *broiled* beef patties between buns and served them to *a demanding crowd*, *which* gulped them down joyously. 一句話就道出了漢堡包的產生過程。用漢語講表達，起碼要用三個分句來完成："在交易會的餐廳里一群等著吃飯的人催促著快上菜，急得一個廚師只

— 23 —

好飛快地把烤熟的牛肉餅夾在面包里端上來應急,那群餓急了的人立刻痛痛快快地大口吃了起來。"

例2： Low productivity rates and a reputation for poor quality and strikes mean *that*, *with* the exception of British Leyland, the major car manufacturers are producing fewer and fewer cars in Britain and importing not only more fully-built cars, but also assembly kits *with* most of high technology parts coming from overseas.

由於英國汽車製造業生產率低,並有產品質量差和罷工多的名聲,除了不列顛萊蘭公司外,主要的汽車生產廠家在英國生產的汽車越來越少。這些廠家不但從國外進口更多整車,而且進口高科技配件。

【分析】這一段只有一句話,負載的信息量卻很大。在漢語中,這麼長的句子是不多見的。翻譯此句必須用五六個分句才行。

例3： *When* I try to understand *what* it is *that* prevents so many Americans from being *as* happy *as* one might expect, it seems to me *that* there are two causes, of *which* one goes much deeper than the other.

為什麼如此眾多的美國人不能如想象中那樣幸福呢? 我認為原因有二,而兩者之間又有深淺之分。

【分析】短短的一句話中就用了七個關係詞和連接詞,漢語句子則少用或不用這類詞,用了反而顯得多餘。

2.介詞運用的差異

介詞是英語中最活躍、最常用的詞類之一,是連接詞、短語、句子和從句的重要手段,英語造句幾乎離不開介詞。而漢語最缺乏的詞類恐怕就是介詞了,僅有的30多個介詞也是源自動詞。在翻譯時往往會造成困難。例如:

例1： She is over 60, but still *with it.* 雖然她已經60多歲了,可穿戴仍然很入時。

【分析】to be with it 是介詞短語,意思是 to know about present ideas and fashions。不了解這個意思,便無從翻譯這個句子。

例2： Scientists believe they *are onto something big.*

科學家確信他們已經有了重大發現。

【分析】要想翻譯好此句,首先要弄清 be onto sth. 的意思。這是個固定的介詞短語，意思是 to know about something or be in a situation that could lead to a good result。

例3：The many colors *of* a rainbow range *from* red *on* the outside *to* violet *on* the inside.

彩虹有多種顏色，外圈兒紅，內圈兒紫。

例4：He had a disconcerting habit *of* expressing contradictory ideas *in* rapid succession.

他有一種令人難堪的習慣：一會兒一個看法，自相矛盾，變幻無常。

例5：This was an intelligently organized and fervent meeting *in* a packed Town Hall, *with* Mr. Strong in the chair.

這是一次精心組織起來的會議。市政廳里濟濟一堂，熱情洋溢，主持會議的是斯特朗先生。

例6：When the factory was first established, the designers and engineers worked long hours *on* meager food, *in* cold mobile homes, *by* dim lamps.

在建廠初期，設計師和工程師吃簡單的食物，住寒冷的簡易房，就著微弱的燈光，長時間地工作。

例7："Coming!" Away she skimmed *over* the lawn, *up* the path, *up* the steps, *across* the pond, and *outside* the gate.

"來啦！"她轉身蹦著跳著跑了，越過草地，跑上小徑，跨過池塘，出了大門。

【分析】從例3到例7的原句中，使用了大量介詞，漢語譯文則必須用動詞來表達。

二、漢譯英中的障礙

漢語的時間順序和邏輯關係常常按照由先到後、由因到果、由假設到推論、由事實到結論這樣的次序排列。漢語中的時態、語態信息的主次關係很少用詞標明，更沒有形態變化。而英語卻正好與此相反，任何語法現象都必須以詞和句子的形態變化明確表示。在漢譯英時，必須首先弄清句子的意思，尤其是暗含的意思。請看下例：

例1：據說這本書已譯成多種語言。

The book *is said to have been translated* into many languages.

例2：我後悔沒有聽她的勸告。

I regret *not having taken* her advice.

例3：全中國各大城市都在興建新賓館。

New hotels *are being built* in all the big cities in China.

例4：他跟我說,到年底他教英語就有30年了。

He told me that by the end of the year he *would have been working* as an English teacher for thirty years.

【分析】例1原句中的被動語態,並沒有用"被"字明確表示,在英語句子里必須用語法手段表示。例2、例3、例4中,漢語句子的時態也不十分明確,但在英語中必須分別表示出來:not having taken(以前未做的事),are being built(正在進行的事),would have been working(間接引語中表示將來要完成的事)。

例5：那個老大娘哭得心都碎了,我問她怎麼了,她說她的錢包讓人偷了,已經一整天沒吃東西了,實在餓極了。

The elderly woman, who was crying as if her heart would break, *said*, when I spoke to her, *that she was very hungry*, because she had had her purse stolen and had no money to buy food for a whole day.

【分析】在英語中,往往重要的信息先說,或用主句來突出,而漢語卻是"按部就班"按時間順序,慢慢道來。這就需要譯者迅速識別哪個是頭等大事,以便在英譯句子中體現出來。這句話的主要意思是:"老大娘說她實在餓極了。"其他成分表示時間、餓的原因等,相對來說比較次要,所以用從句表示。

例6：我把信寫好了,經理看了看,簽上名,遞給秘書,秘書把信放在文件夾里。

Looking briefly at the letter, which I wrote, *the manager signed his name and passed it to his secretary*, who put it into a folder.

【分析】這句話的主要意思是:"經理在信上簽了名,遞給秘書。"至於誰寫的信,秘書把信放哪了,都是次要信息。

例7：這棵樹已經有三百多年的樹齡了，樹干直徑竟有兩米，枝葉繁茂，是這座林子里唯一沒有在那場大風中被刮倒的樹。

This 300-year-old *tree* with a trunk of two meters in diameter and flourishing foliages *is the only tree that survived in the windstorm.*

【分析】這句話主要說的是"這棵樹是這座林子里唯一沒有在那場大風中被刮倒的樹"，應作主句。其他成分都是描繪樹的樣子和樹齡，要用分詞和介詞短語來表達。

例8：在臺上臺下都一樣，這位演員姿態神情也是可欣賞的：說話不疾不徐，目不他瞬，臉上泛著笑意。

On stage or off, *this actor was a sight to enjoy*, talking in perfect ease, looking at you with a smile on his face.

【分析】這句話的中心意思是："這位演員姿態神情也是可欣賞的。"其他信息都是描述演員姿態、神情的細節，用分詞或從句來表述。

例9：這個演員家隔壁住的鄰居有個保姆，每天清晨灑掃庭院，必聽他唱念，居然也學會了幾出戲。

The maidservant of the actor's next-door neighbor even *learned to sing a few operas* by listening to the actor rehearsing every morning when she was doing the daily cleaning.

【分析】這句話主要說的是"這個保姆居然也學會了幾出戲"。至於如何學的和什麼時候學的，都在次要位置。

例10：他被剝奪了權力之後，被軟禁在家15年，唯一的自由是打打高爾夫球。

He *was put under house arrest* for 15 years and *allowed only to play gulf* sometimes, having been deprived of his power.

【分析】雖然漢語句子里一開頭就講"他被剝奪了權力之後"，但只不過是時間狀語從句，要放在句尾，而主要的事是他現在的狀況："被軟禁在家"和"打高爾夫球"，這些必須首先講明。

例11：我們1959年來到美國。後來，從報紙上看到家鄉連續三年遭了災，心里真難受。

We *were dismayed* while reading of the natural calamities that followed one another for three years in my hometown after we came to America in 1959.

【分析】原句是典型的流水句,主要信息是"心里真難受",放在最後,但在英語里卻要先說。

綜上所述,不難看出,翻譯其實是一種思維方式的轉換,是按照譯文讀者的語言習慣,克服漢英語言之間語法結構差異所造成的障礙,進行必要轉換的過程。改變的是原語語法,保留的是原文意思。

必須指出的是,雖然漢英這兩種語言存在很大差異,我們絕不能把這種意合與形合、隱性結構與顯性結構的區別絕對化,也就是說,漢語的主要特徵是意合和隱性,但並不是沒有形合和顯性。最近 20 年來,漢語"歐化"趨勢加快,尤其在英譯漢文章中,甚至在漢語原作中,關係詞、連接詞、介詞等連接手段也在廣泛運用。但是在大量的歷史文獻、文學著作中,意合和隱性仍是漢語的主要特徵,漢英翻譯中的障礙依然存在,譯者仍然要進行必要的轉換。因此,對比、分析、歸納英漢語之間的差異,仍是翻譯學的重要任務。

思考題

1. 在漢英互譯時,譯者首先要考慮的問題是什麼? 是語法還是詞匯?
2. 有人說漢語的句子結構是"竹竿"形的,而英語句子是"葡萄藤"形的。這些特點主要體現在哪些方面?

第四章　結構轉換

　　由於漢英兩種語言的語法結構存在較大差異,翻譯時必須進行必要的轉換。具體來講,哪些成分需要轉換? 轉換的依據又是什麼? 這裡需要運用一個語言學理論:表層結構(surface structure) 和深層結構 (deep structure) 的關係問題。

　　我們在交際中看到或聽到的話語,即語言的書面形式或聲音形式,其實只是語言的表層結構,而深層結構,也就是作者或講話者的意圖,在他們講話之前就已經形成了。一句話的表層結構代表或不一定代表語言的深層結構。人們是通過表層結構感知深層結構的。講話的過程就是把腦中的深層結構進行" 編碼"(to encode),以話語形式表述出來的過程。聽者或讀者是按照在長期的交際中形成的"代碼"來對聽到或讀到的話語進行"解碼"(to decode) 的,也就是理解深層意思。而譯者具有雙重任務:先對原文進行"解碼",然後用譯文語言再度"編碼"。即通過原文的表層結構,掌握深層結構,再用譯文的表層結構轉述這一深層結構。這個過程可通過以下模式說明:

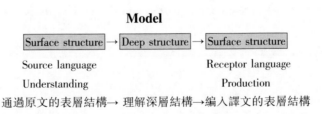

Model

| Surface structure | → | Deep structure | → | Surface structure |

Source language　　　　　　　　　　　Receptor language

Understanding　　　　　　　　　　　　Production

通過原文的表層結構→ 理解深層結構→編入譯文的表層結構

　　所有能夠達意的句子應該只有一個深層結構,一個或多個表層結構。例如,表示"非常憤怒",在漢英語言中就有很多表達方式:

例 1：

Chinese	English
火冒三丈,怒不可遏, 怒發衝冠,怒火中燒, 怒氣衝天,怒氣填胸, 怒形於色, 氣不打一處來, 氣得他直上莊稼火	wild with anger mad with anger beside oneself with rage lose control of one's temper fly into a passion blow one's top go up in the air go through the roof set up one's bristles

　　在互譯中,這些表層結構雖然存在細微差別,但只要認準"非常憤怒"這一深層結構,翻譯就可大體完成,推敲細微的意思是翻譯的第二步。

例 2：儘管這個學生有不少缺點,但我還是喜歡她。

　　這句話可英譯成多種句式或表層結構。例如：

a. I like this student *for* all her faults.

b. I like this student *in spite of* her faults.

c. I like this student *none the less for* her faults.

d. I do *not* like this student *the less for* her faults.

e. The student has many faults, *but* I like her *all the same.*

f. The student has many faults, *but none the less* I like her.

g. The student has many faults, *but* I do *not* like her *the less.*

　　如果一個表層結構含有兩個深層結構,這句話就是歧義句,就很容易譯錯,例如：

例 3：The policeman rushed into the Clock Tower and found the thief *out*.

a. 警察衝進鐘樓,找到了那個小偷。

b. 警察衝進鐘樓,發現那個小偷已經溜走了。

例 4：He turned *out* a swindler.

　　a. 他原來是個騙子。　　　　　　　b. 他把一個騙子趕走了。

例 **5**：We left Tom to paint the room.
　　　a. 我們讓湯姆留下來粉刷房子。　　b. 我們離開湯姆去粉刷房子。

例 **6**：The chicken is too cold to eat.
　　　a. 鷄已經凉了,不好吃了。　　　b. 這只小鷄凍得都吃不了食兒了。

例 **7**：The love of a father was strong in him.
　　　a. 他從心里感到了父親對他強烈的愛。
　　　b. 他心里充滿了強烈的父愛。

例 **8**：We answered the questions on the paper.
　　　a. 我們回答了報紙上登的所有問題。
　　　b. 我們以書面形式回答了所有的問題。

例 **9**：看了這部電影以後,別的電影就不必看了。
　　　a. You've seen this movie, and you've seen all.
　　　b. If you see this movie, you'll find other movies are not worth seeing.

　　如果我們在讀原文時沒有理解深層意思,只翻譯表層結構,譯文就有可能不通,或不能忠實於原文。例如:

例 **10**：That guy really ***knows a thing or two.***
　　　〔誤〕那家伙真是略知一二。　　〔正〕那家伙真是**見多識廣**。

例 **11**：This is ***the last place*** where I expected to meet you.
　　　〔誤〕這是我想見到你的最後一個地方。
　　　〔正〕**萬萬沒想到**會在這個地方碰到你!

例 **12**：He has got hold of ***the wrong end of the stick.***
　　　〔誤〕他的棍子拿倒了。　　　〔正〕他完全**搞錯**了。

例 **13**：You look sad. ***Don't tell me*** you're out of a job again.
　　　〔誤〕你看上去挺難過,別告訴我你又失業了!
　　　〔正〕你看上去挺難過,**難道**你又失業了!

在翻譯界，很多學者常常討論譯文的"重寫"問題(rewriting)。所謂"重寫"，並不是漫無邊際的再創作，而是當原文中的表現法與譯文讀者的文化不相符時，譯者對語言結構進行的整體調整，以使譯文符合讀者的表達習慣。這種整體調整是建立在局部結構轉換的基礎上的。具體地講，英譯漢時，需對英語結構緊湊的句式進行分切、重組，轉換成漢語流水句；漢譯英時，需對漢語詞組和分句的意思、功能、邏輯進行分析，以確定英譯文句子的主語和謂語，同時添加必要的關聯詞，構成層次分明的"立體"句式。

一、英譯漢中的結構轉換

1. 拆句重組

英語中有些嚴謹的結構無法再現於漢語譯文，只能把原句拆開，重新組合。有時英語中的一個字就要譯成一個分句。例如：

例1：This is a matter concerning the welfare of factory workers and any comment on it should ***appropriately*** come from the trade union.

這是一個有關工人福利的問題，對這個問題的任何意見都應當由工會來發表，**這才是適宜的**。

例2：The young man was ***naturally*** proud of his beautiful penmanship.

這小伙子以寫一筆好字為傲，**這是很自然的**。

例3：The prisoners are permitted to receive parcels from their family and write ***censored*** letters.

犯人可以接收家人送來的包裹，也允許寫信，**不過信要經過檢查**。

例4：The former president of the university cannot ***politely*** turn down the invitation to the celebration of the university's 45th anniversary.

老校長若拒絕參加建校 45 周年紀念活動，**在禮貌上是說不過去的**。

例5：The dean of the department cannot ***responsibly*** stay aloof from the students' difficulties.

系主任如果對學生的困難不聞不問，**那就是沒有盡到責任**。

例 6：The farmers are *justifiably* proud of their bumper harvest after the drought.

農民們為他們戰勝旱災後奪取的大豐收而自豪，**這是合乎情理的**。

例 7：They, *not surprisingly*, did not do any preparations for the project.

他們對這個項目沒作任何準備工作，**這是不足為奇的**。

例 8：The school leaders might have spoken with *understandable* pride of their outstanding graduates.

校領導在談到他們的優秀畢業生時，也許有些自豪，**這是可以理解的**。

2. 補充說明

用漢語說明抽象概念時，如果不加上較為具體的詞進行補充說明，讀者會覺得句子不完整。

例 1：All the people were exasperated by his *irresponsibility.*

大家都被他那種不負責任的**做法**激怒了。

例 2：No one is satisfied with his *favoritism* in his work.

對他在工作中表現出來的徇私**作風**誰都不滿意。

例 3：We were all greatly moved by his *selflessness.*

我們都被他的無私**精神**深深打動了。

例 4：The pharmacologists are making a careful study of the *allergy* of the medicine.

藥理學家們正在認真研究這種藥的過敏**反應**。

例 5：His *arrogance* sent him into isolation and helplessness.

他的傲慢**態度**使他孤立無援。

例 6：The hall was filled with *sobriety* with several priests sitting on the stage.

臺上坐著幾個牧師，使大廳充滿了莊重的**氣氛**。

例 7：Her *jealousy* is the cause of her poor health.

她的忌妒**心理**是她疾病纏身的根源。

例 8：Her *indifference* kept many friends away from her.

她的冷漠**態度**讓很多朋友離她而去。

例 9：It's more expensive than it was last time but not as good.

價錢比上次的高，但**質量卻比上次的**差。

例 10：The fan, with its modern, elegant, bright, and harmoniously colored design, is an excellent electrical household appliance for cooling purposes on hot summer days.

本電扇**款式**新穎，**造型**大方，**色彩**鮮艷，**色澤**和諧，是炎炎夏日消暑納涼的家電精品。

3. 省略多餘詞語

省略主語：根據漢語習慣，英語句子泛指的人稱代詞做主語時，主語在譯文中要省略。

例 1：*We* live and learn. 活到老，學到老。

例 2：*You* can never tell. 很難說。

例 3：Rest in itself is not enough, *one* can never get real rest without a peaceful mind.

光休息是不夠的，心不淨是休息不好的。

省略做主語的人稱代詞：前句出現一個主語後句仍為同一主語，譯文中不必出現。

例 4：He was thin and haggard and *he* looked miserable.

他消瘦而憔悴，看上去一副受苦相。

例 5： It's the way I am, and try as *I* might, *I* haven't been able to change it.

我就是這個脾氣，幾次想改，也沒改掉。

例 6： He was well-favored, bright, a good dancer, and a fine tennis player. *He* was an asset at any party. *He* was lavish with flowers and expensive boxes of chocolate.

他英俊，聰明，舞跳得不錯，網球也打得很好。什麼聚會都少不了他。鮮花和高價巧克力任意買來送人。

省略物主代詞：

例 7： He is a good friend that speaks well of us behind *our* backs.

在背後贊揚你的人才是真正的好朋友。

例 8： The old professor put *his* pen down, crossed *his* hands behind his neck, and turned *his* face up to the ceiling.

老教授放下筆，兩手交叉著放在脖子後面，抬起頭望著天花板。

例 9： She went, with *her* neat figure, and *her* sober womanly steps, down the dark street.

她順著黑暗的街道走去，顯出利落勻稱的身材，邁著端莊女人的步子。

例 10： He shrugged *his* shoulders, shook *his* head, cast up *his* eyes, but said nothing.

他聳聳肩，搖搖頭，兩眼看天，一句話不說。

二、漢譯英中的結構轉換

漢英翻譯過程中的結構轉換與英漢翻譯的結構轉換正好相反：首要的任務是確定主語，然後確定主要謂語，然後完成其他細微的轉換。

1. 確定主語

由於漢語的句子以主旨意思為中心，只要能達意，有沒有主語，主語的位置如何並不重要。例如：

例 1：我們那時候不知談些什麼,只記得閏土很高興,說是上城之後,見了許多沒見過的東西。

(魯迅:《故鄉》)

I don't know what we talked of then, but *I* remember that Runtu was in high spirits, saying that since *he* had come to town *he* had seen many new things.

(楊憲益,戴乃迭　譯)

例 2：過分謙虛並不太好。

It's not good to be over-modest.

例 3：晚飯十個人一桌,怎麼樣?

For dinner, is it OK to set ten for each table?

例 4：菜點了嗎? Have you ordered?

例 5：老師不來,解決不了問題。

We cannot make any decision on it without the teacher.

例 6：有博士文憑不一定有真才實學。

A PhD does not necessarily mean he is well-learned.

例 7：他的文章寫得寓意深長,受到同行的贊許。

The profundity of his essays has won him the praise of his peers.

例 8：有意見就提,這沒有錯。

There is nothing wrong to complain.

2. 確定主要謂語

漢語中使用最多、最為活躍的詞類是動詞,一句話常常包含好幾個動詞。而英語句子只能有一個主要的謂語動詞,其他所要表達的動作要以介詞、分詞或從句來表示。例如:

例 1: 我冒了嚴寒,回到相隔兩千餘里,別了二十餘年的故鄉去。

魯迅:《故鄉》

Braving the bitter cold, I *traveled* more than seven hundred miles back to the old home I had left over twenty years before.

（楊憲益,戴乃迭　譯）

例 2: 學生犯了錯,作為老師你不管就是你的不對了。

It's your fault as a teacher not to do anything for the student who has done wrong.

例 3: 作為學生,每天不外乎看書、上課、做作業。

As a student, you do nothing more than reading, attending lectures and doing homework.

例 4: 生病並不可怕,怕就怕大夫不能對症下藥。

Don't panic when you're sick, but the wrong medicine the doctor prescribes is something you have to watch out for.

例 5: 他給我發了短信,請我到他老家去玩兒。

He texted me, inviting me to visit his hometown.

例 6: 這個公園世界聞名,吸引了很多外賓前來遊覽。

Being a famous park in the world, it attracts many foreign visitors.

例 7: 天下著大雪,他還在校園里散步。

He is even taking a walk on campus in spite of the heavy snow.

例 8: 刮了一夜大風,氣溫降了 10℃。

The strong wind that blew all last night brought down the temperature by 10℃.

例 9: 這樣的事天天有,沒什麼稀奇。

This is just a daily occurrence, nothing extraordinary.

例 10: 夕陽西下,滿天彩霞。

The sun set, leaving the sky in a riot of rosy clouds.

例 11：我們只坐了三個半小時的火車,就到了太原。

　　· It only took us three and half hours to get to Taiyuan by train.

　　· The train ride to Taiyuan only took us three and half hours.

例 12：他的襯衣多得一輩子都穿不完。

　　He has more shirts than he needs to last him all his life.

例 13：公司資金不足,人手短缺,管理混亂,只得關門。

　　Beset with many problems such as shortages of funds and manpower, poor management, the company will have to close.

3. 按照英語習慣組句

例 1：他們用根繩子勒住了一個鬼子的喉嚨。

　　They caught a Japanese devil **by the throat** with a rope.

例 2：總統很高興地一個接一個地拍了拍那些小孩的頭。

　　One by one the President happily patted the kids **on the head.**

例 3：警察拍了拍小偷的背,說:"跟我走一趟吧。"

　　The policeman tapped the thief **on the shoulder**, saying, "Come with me."

例 4：你怎麼能嫁給他? 論年齡,他可是你兒子輩兒的人。

　　How can you decide to marry him? He is **no older than** your son.

　　在英語中,動詞加-er 是常見的表達方式,是帶有很強動感的名詞,這個用法表示一個人的能力和特點,要比動詞自然、簡潔。請看下例:

例 5：她可真能吃!

　　She is a real **guzzler.**

例 6：他歌唱得好,毛筆字寫得也不錯。

　　He is a **good** singer and excellent **calligrapher.**

例 7：能扮演這種角色的有好幾個人。

There were various possible *players* for the role.

例 8：這位老獵人滑雪滑得好。

The old hunter is a good *skier.*

例 9：我恐怕教不了你游泳，我弟弟比我**教得好**。

I'm afraid I can't teach you swimming.　My brother is a *better teacher* than I.

例 10：他不抽烟，可他爸爸卻一支接一支**抽個不停**。

He is a *non-smoker*, but his father is a *chain-smoker.*

例 11：他**有酒量**。

He is a great *drinker.*

例 12：他這個人真**能說**。

He is a great *talker.*

例 13：他**酷愛**古典音樂。

He is an ardent *lover* of classic music.

例 14：這個小學生文章**寫**得不錯。

This pupil is a good *writer.*

例 15：他曾經**統治**那個地區長達20年之久。

He was the *ruler* of that region for as long as 20 years.

例 16：他**教書**已經30年了。

He is a *teacher* of 30 years.

例 17：這個工廠長期**虧損**。

This factory is a chronic *money loser.*

例 18：我同**生長在南方的人**合不來。

I don't usually get on well with *southerners.*

4. 壓縮調整

例 1： 他來到華盛頓，**就國際形勢來說**，時機正合適。

He arrived in Washington at a ripe moment *internationally*.

例 2： 我們老師沒有表露自己的感覺，只是觀察、思索，**這是他的特點**。

Characteristically, our teacher concealed his feelings and watched and learned.

例 3： 他滿以為問題會自然而然地得到解決，**這是不合情理的事**。

Illogically, he expected the problem can be solved naturally.

例 4： 他感到語法是語言的主要支柱，**這個想法非常正確**。

He has a *correct* thought that grammar is the backbone of a language.

例 5： 他在 50 歲時還想出國深造，**可是希望落空了**。

At the age of 50, he hoped *in vain* to go abroad to get further education.

例 6： 他的**身體**雖弱，但**思維**健全。

He is *physically* weak but *mentally* sound.

　　以上所表述的只是漢英互譯中結構轉換的一部分，其他更為細微的轉換要視所譯文本的具體語境而定。詳細的轉換還要在後幾章中論述。

思考題

1. 在翻譯中為什麼要進行結構轉換？
2. 語法結構轉換是否與再創作為同一概念？

第五章　直譯與意譯

是直譯還是意譯？這個問題爭論了幾乎一個世紀。近 20 年，這個爭論又升級為異化和歸化的爭論，並且有愈演愈烈的趨勢。究竟什麼叫異化？為什麼要異化？歸化的目的又何在？這是一個需要正本清源的問題。直譯和意譯主要是具體的翻譯方法的問題，而異化和歸化則是針對文化差異的翻譯策略問題。

一、直譯和意譯的必要性

翻譯家 Newmark 是直譯的倡導者，但他從來沒有提倡過詞對詞的死譯，而是強調"如果直譯能確保在內容上、在語言的實際運用中，譯文與原文是對等時，直譯就是正確的、不必著意回避的。"（ My thesis, however, is that literal translation is correct and must not be avoided, *if it secures referential and pragmatic equivalence to the original.* ）"雖然大多數語言在詞匯方面有著奇怪的差異，但只要兩種語言出現文化共同點，對一個普通事物就可以進行一對一的直譯。"（ Further, a common object will usually have one-to-one literal translation *if there is cultural overlap*, though most languages have strange lexical gaps. ）

直譯法就是在符合譯文語言規則的情況下，既保持原文的內容，又不改變其修辭特點（如句式、形象比喻、民族或地方特色等）的翻譯方法。

其實，我國長期的翻譯實踐早已證明，直譯的方式已經極大地豐富了我們的現代漢語。現代漢語中的許多詞匯都是從梵文佛經中音譯過來的。"我們日常流行的許多用語，如世界、如實、實際、平等、現行、剎那、清規戒律、相對、絕對等都來自佛教語匯。如果真要徹底擯棄佛教文化的話，恐怕他們連話都說不周全了。"（趙樸初，1991）

現代漢語中源自英語的詞匯實例也不勝枚舉：

1	black market	黑市
2	to show one's cards	攤牌
3	dollar diplomacy	金元外交
4	pillar industry	支柱產業
5	Time is money.	時間就是金錢。
6	packed like sardines	擠得像沙丁魚罐頭
7	a gentleman's agreement	君子協定
8	an olive branch	橄欖枝
9	the most-favored-nation clause	最惠國條款
10	shuttle diplomacy	穿梭外交
11	Blood is thicker than water.	血濃於水

　　隨著國際交往的日益頻繁,漢語也正極快地走向世界。這些年英語也吸收了大量的漢語詞匯:

1	工夫	Kong Fu
2	番茄醬	Ketchup
3	太極拳	Taijiquan
4	大白菜	Bok choy
5	鐵飯碗	Iron Rice Bowl
6	一國兩制	one country, two systems
7	世界之窗	Window of the World
8	"豆腐渣"工程	construction project with building materials like bean dregs

　　著名翻譯家劉重德對不適當的直譯有很到位的論述:"至於譯文中有時出現的翻譯腔(translationese)倒是應該避免和克服的語病,有人把這種語病完全歸咎於歐化或直譯,筆者認為這種指責不夠公允,恰當。翻譯腔的產生,如果一定要牽連上歐化或直譯,那麼只能說是歐化或直譯的失度或過度。"現在流行的不自然、不流暢,甚至令人聽而生厭的彆腳翻譯就是過度異化的結果。

　　一種語言表達一種思想,常常採用某種比喻或其他修辭手法,使語言形象、生動、富有感染力。直譯的目的就是為了保留原作手法,因而達到與原文近似的效果。但直譯是以確保譯文讀者很快理解原作內容為前提的。否則只能意譯。例如:

例 1：The teenagers don't invite Bob to their parties because he is a ***wet blanket***.

這些年輕人從不邀請鮑勃參加聚會，因為他是個**讓人掃興的人**。

例 2：All right, I blame myself. But it's the last time. We were ***cat's paws***, that's all.

得了，怪我自己瞎了眼，可是我再也不干了。我們**上了人家的當**，沒別的。

例 3：To ***break the ice***, Ted spoke of his interest in mountain climbing, and they soon had a conversation going.

為了**打破沉默**，泰德說自己對爬山有興趣，這樣他們很快就交談起來。

例 4：She ***was born with a silver spoon in her mouth***; she thinks she can do what she likes.

她**出身高貴**，認為凡事都可隨心所欲。

例 5：***The die was cast***, he could not go back.

事已決定，不容翻悔。

例 6：Paula didn't need any lessons when it comes to ***office politics***.

說到**同事之間的明爭暗鬥**，葆拉可算是無師自通。

例 7：I'd rather take care of the ***stomachs*** of the living than the glory of the dead in ***the form of the stone memorials***.

—Nobel

我寧可關心生者的**溫飽**，也不願為死者**樹碑立傳**。

——諾貝爾

　　意譯法就是在要想保持原文的內容，就不能兼顧其修辭特點的情況下，不得不改變說法才能把作者原意表達出來時採取的方法。以下例句就必須採取意譯的方式。

　　英譯漢：

	原文	意譯
1	technical know-how	專業技術
2	talk shop all the time	三句話不離本行
3	a land of honey and milk	魚米之鄉
4	Penny wise, pound foolish.	小處節約，大處浪費。 小事聰明，大事糊塗。

漢譯英：

	原文	意譯
1	五湖四海	all corners of the country
2	拳頭產品	competitive products / key products
3	換血	personnel reshuffle
4	下海	get a job in commerce
5	上岸	quite the job in commerce, resume one's old profession
6	充電	update one's knowledge
7	吃不了兜著走	be in serious trouble
8	這只是頭疼醫頭，腳疼醫腳。	This is merely makeshift for a solution.
9	知人知面不知心	You never know what the next person thinks about.
10	這山望著那山高	Grass is always greener on the other side of the hill.
11	打開天窗說亮話	Let's speak frankly.
12	木已成舟	What is done cannot be undone.

二、異化與歸化的目的性

　　對這個問題 Newmark 作過明確的論述："恰當的直譯本身必須具備表達生動的條件。如果譯文中顯現出原文的干擾，這必須是譯者有意使然。在旅遊景點介紹中出現輕微的翻譯腔會使景點顯得更有魅力，就像給譯文詞語增添了異地色彩……如果譯者對譯文中的原文干擾渾然不知，其中必有誤譯。"（A good literal translation must be effective in its own right. If it shows SL[①]interference, that must be ***by the translator's conscious decision.*** Some mild translationese in a tourist brochure has gentle charm, like the local color of a transferred word... ***The translator unconscious of SL interference is always at fault.***）

　　魯迅主張直譯。雖然當時還沒有異化這個提法，但同屬一個概念。他這樣做的目的是：在介紹外國思想以供借鑑的同時，還要通過譯文改造當時中國的語言。他是主張"寧信而不順"的，他認為："這樣的譯本，不但在輸入新的內容，也在輸入

---

① SL：source language.

新的表現法。中國的文或話,法子實在太不精密了⋯⋯這語法的不精密,就在證明思路的不精密,換一句話,就是腦筋有些糊塗。倘若永遠用著糊塗話,即使讀的時候,滔滔而下,但歸根結底,所得的還是一個糊塗的影子。要醫這病,我認為只好陸續吃一點苦,裝進異樣的句法去,古的、外省外府的、外國的,後來便可以據為己有。"這話乍聽起來,有點刺耳,好像有損於中國傳統文化,但細想一下,魯迅對我們的語言是"愛之深,責之切"的。

公認的異化論創立者 Lawrence Venuti 給異化翻譯法下了經典的定義:"保持外國文本中的語言和文化特點,使讀者有出國之感。"(to register the linguistic and cultural difference of the foreign text, sending the readers abroad.)

如果翻譯的目的是把中國的語言特色介紹給英譯文讀者,就完全可以採用異化策略,例如:

例1: 去設埋伏我們都沒有信心,想他一定在昨天晚上早就溜了,今天去也是**瞎子點燈白費蠟**。

(曲波:《林海雪原》)

We had no confidence in today's ambush because we were sure he had escaped last night. It seemed *as useless as a blind man lighting a candle.*

(S. Shapiro 譯)

例2: 蔣介石是**泥菩薩過江,自身難保**。

(周立波:《暴風驟雨》)

Even Chiang Kai-shek can't save himself any more than *a clay idol can save itself while swimming across a river.*

(S. Shapiro 譯)

例3: "噯!我也知道艱難的,但俗話說:'**瘦死的駱駝比馬大**。'憑你怎麼樣,**您老拔一根汗毛比我們的腰還粗呢!**"

"Ah, I know what difficulties are. But '*A starved camel is bigger than a horse.*' No matter how, *a hair from your body is thicker than our waist.*"

(楊憲益,戴乃迭 譯)

例4: 同他談判你要格外小心,他可是出了名的**笑面虎**。

You must be very careful to negotiate with him, he is well-known as a "*smiling tiger*".

例 5：這個教授學識淵博，可不善言談，講課就像**茶壺里煮餃子，好吃倒不出來**。

This professor is very learned, but he is not very articulate in his lectures, *like boiling jiaozi in a teapot, it's difficult to get it out.*

例 6：鄰里之間不該為**鷄毛蒜皮**的小事爭吵。

As neighbors, we should not argue over *chicken feathers and garlic skins.*

例 7：讀他的書簡直是**味同嚼蠟**。

His book is too boring to read, *as tasteless as chewing wax.*

例 8：要想讓工人好好干活兒，就得給人家漲工資，你總不能**又要馬兒跑，又要馬兒不吃草吧**。

You must raise the workers' wages, if you want them to work hard. How can you *want a horse to run fast and not let it graze*?

　　但是在很多情況下，直譯或者異化是根本行不通的，我們必須採取意譯或歸化的譯法才能傳達原文的意思。

英漢譯例：

例 9：That theory *doesn't hold water.*
　　　這個理論**站不住腳**。

例 10：*A wreck on shore is a beacon at sea.*
　　　　前車之覆，後車之鑒。

例 11：Our appeal remained *a dead letter.*
　　　我們的呼吁**如石沉大海**。

例 12：She was, to be sure, a girl who excited the emotion, but I was not the one *to let my heart rule my head.*
　　　她確實是一個令人動情的姑娘，不過我不是一個**讓感情支配理智的人**。

漢英譯例：

例 13：明天就是春節了,咱們應該**改善改善生活**。

Tomorrow is Spring Festive, why don't *we have a good meal*?

例 14：這個會我可不去,我只不過是個**群眾**。

I'm not going to that meeting, because I'm not a *government official*.

例 15：這兩個人**一個唱紅臉,一個唱白臉**,你誰都別相信。

One of them is playing the nice guy, *the other the villain.* Don't you believe either of them.

例 16：你們別笑,**老鼠拉木鍁──大頭還在後邊呢!**

Don't laugh; *the best is yet to come*!

例 17：他要是問我,我給他來個**徐庶進操營──一言不發**。

If he asks me, I'll *hold my tongue to begin with*.

凡事都要有度,如果過分強調譯文或原文的語言和文化,即過度歸化或異化,結果會使譯文讀者感到莫名其妙或索然無味。例如,David Hawkes 對曹雪芹《紅樓夢》中的"紅"字處理,就完全是毫無意義的歸化譯法:

《紅樓夢》　A Dream of Golden Days　怡紅院　　the House of Green Delights
悼紅軒　　Nostalgia Studio　　怡紅公子　Green Boy

Hawkes 這樣做的目的可能是怕 red 一詞經常用於貶義,容易引起讀者的負面聯想,但是,這種以西方文化代替中國文化的做法大大損害了這部偉大文學作品的藝術價值。

一個過度異化的譯例是賽珍珠對《水滸傳》中某些稱謂的翻譯。例如,冒充李逵的李鬼管他的妻子叫"大嫂",她管丈夫叫"大哥"。賽珍珠分別譯做 elder sister 和 elder brother。讀者看了以後肯定弄不清這兩個人是什麼關係。林衝對別人稱自己的妻子為"拙荊",賽珍珠把它譯成 that stupid one who is my wife,看到這里,讀者會誤認為林衝根本不愛自己的妻子。

以下的歸化譯法也是不恰當的:

Talk of the devil, the devil comes.　　說曹操,曹操就到。
The losses were caused by your carelessness.　　你這是大意失荊州。

Beauty is in the eye of the beholder. 　　　　　　　情人眼里出西施。

　　中英翻譯中的直譯與意譯、異化與歸化是互為補充的兩種翻譯策略。在翻譯實踐中，既有必要，又要適度。過分依賴與拒不接受，都有損於我們的翻譯效果。使用的標準是按照譯語的基本詞匯和語法規律來遣詞造句、布局成篇。一切以譯文讀者的接受與理解為原則，努力在內容上求信，在敘述上求達，在風格上求美，使我們的翻譯工作不斷改進。

思考題

1. 直譯或異化的目的是什麼?
2. 有人主張"能直譯則直譯，不能直譯才意譯"，也有人認為"絕對的直譯是不存在的，翻譯都是意譯，只是程度不同罷了"。你同意哪種觀點?

第二部分　句子翻譯

第六章　主語的確定

第七章　連動式的處理

第八章　從屬信息的翻譯

第九章　虛擬語氣的翻譯

第十章　静態和動態的翻譯

第十一章　被動語態的翻譯

第十二章　名詞的翻譯

第十三章　選詞的技巧

第六章　主語的確定

　　多年來，很多翻譯家和翻譯理論學者從不同的角度對漢英翻譯中主語的確定進行過論述。他們幾乎一致認為，中國人和西方人的思維方式不同、中英文的語法形式不同決定了中西兩種不同的講話習慣。兩種講話習慣的差異在漢英翻譯當中如何確定主語方面表現得尤為突出。漢語是意合語言，重意念，輕形式，講究言必達意、述則明了，因此總是顯得靈活、多變，主語的作用並不突出。英語是形合語言，重形式，講邏輯，講究形式明確、表述嚴謹，各種語法成分都要各司其職，而主語則是整個句子的"綱"，是最重要的部分。例如：

　　老黃老了，人稱"黃老"。老啦，沒辦法，吃過晚飯，看了點電視新聞，有些迷糊了，打算洗個臉，泡泡腳，上床尋夢去。

　　門鈴一聲響，來了客人。從不謝客，禮當接待。忙把襪子穿上，整冠而出。來客紅光滿面，一開口就知道是遠客。

（樓適夷：《夜間來客》）

　　Mr. Huang was old. *People* addressed him as "Respected Mr. Huang". Being old, *he* easily got tired and could not help it. After supper, having watched some news on the TV, *he* began to feel sleepy, so he went about washing his face and feet before going to bed.

　　Suddenly *the doorbell* rang, announcing the arrival of a visitor. As *Mr. Huang* had never refused any visitor before, *this one* should be received with courtesy too. Quickly putting his socks back on and smoothing his hair, *he* hurried to the door, and encountered by a man with a fat glowing face. By the first word he uttered *Mr. Huang* was sure this man from a far-off place.

（劉世聰　譯）

　　在上例的第二段中，出現了兩個主語：老黃和來客，在原文的表述中，不必特意說明誰"從不謝客"，誰"禮當接待"，誰"忙把襪子穿上，整冠而出"，誰"一開口就知道是遠客"。但在英譯文中，誰是動作的發出者要交代得清清楚楚。

　　漢英翻譯的第一步就是確定主語，邁出了這一步，整個句子翻譯就有了眉目。只有確定了主語，整個英語句子才有了框架，走下一步就比較順利了。但是，初學漢譯英的人在這一步上往往躊躇不決，像走入迷宮，很長時間理不出個頭緒，找不到主語或很難確定合適的主語。例如：

　　好不容易找到一個車位，費了半天勁卻發現，地方太小技術太差停不進去，多煩人。

　　雖然這句話中暗含的主語是"我"，但漢語不明說，再加上又出現了"地方"、"技術"等名詞，使翻譯更為複雜。但在英譯文中只要找到主語，其他問題便可迎刃而解。

　　It took me a long time to get a parking place, but only to find the place was too crowded to drive in especially with my limited driving skills, which was a very annoying experience.

　　下面我們具體歸納一下在確立主語時可能遇到的幾種典型情況。

一、補充主語

　　漢語句子中最重要的成分是主題，主語往往不突出，只要能把事情說清楚，能讓人聽懂所要表達的意思，有沒有主語，用什麼來充當主語，並不重要。有很多句子是無主句，在譯成英語時，必須加上主語，例如：

例1：進了學校南門就是教學主樓。
The major lecture building is just inside the south gate of the school.

例2：有教無類。
Education for all.

例3：不看不知道，一看嚇一跳。
The mere sight of it gave me a shock.

例4：餓了吃糠甜如蜜。
Hunger is the best relish for food.

例 5：禮拜六,早起也行,晚起也行。

You don't have to get up early as usual on Saturday.

例 6：冷嗎,外頭?

Is it cold outside?

例 7：來中國投資既有機遇又有風險。

    ·Investing in China means opportunities and risks.

    ·There are opportunities and risks involved in investing in China.

    在以上例子中,"進了、有、一看、餓了、早起、晚起、投資"都是動詞,但並不表示動作。另外,幾乎什麼詞都可以在漢語句子中做主語,但在英譯時,必須選定名詞或有名詞性質的詞做主語,這就必須把這些動詞以名詞形式譯出來。如在句中找不到,就必須根據上下文補充一個主語,如例 5 和例 6 中的 you 和 it。

二、變換主語

    有時雖然漢語句子中有主語,但譯成英語時卻不能詞對詞地譯成主語,因為不符合英語語言的邏輯關係和講話習慣。例如:

例 1：2008 年五月那地方發生了強烈地震。

A devastating earthquake shook/hit/struck that region in May 2008.

例 2：海南出產香蕉。

Bananas grow in Hainan Province.

例 3：這幅畫越看越叫人喜歡。

The more you look at this picture, the more you'll like it.

例 4：我們的朋友遍天下。

We have friends all over the world.

例 5：機器少了兩顆螺絲釘。

Two screws are missing from the machine.

例 6：這次戰役是中國人民反抗日本侵略的第一次勝利。

  The victory of the campaign was the first ever won by the Chinese people in their struggle against Japanese invasion.

  如果把"2008 年 5 月,海南,這幅畫,我們的朋友,機器,這次戰役"譯做主語,下一步翻譯就無法進行,即便是勉強譯出句子,也是不符合英語講話習慣的中式英語。以例 4 為例,如果把"我們的朋友遍天下"這句充滿自豪感的口號譯成 Our friends are all over the world. 儘管語法正確,意思重心卻發生了偏差,好像是在回答 "Where are your friends?"這個問題,就失去了口號的功能。

三、識別隱形主語

  有時,**漢語中的主語好像"暗藏"在某處,譯者必須用心識別,才能確定主語。**如果找錯了,就會出現中式英語。以下例句就不易找到主語。

例 1：這個地區局勢不穩,根源是有外國駐軍。
  · The cause of the instability in this region is the foreign military presence.
  · The presence of foreign troops in the area is the cause of its instability.

例 2：李老師這麼一個老實人,怎麼會衝你發火?
  How could a good-natured man like Mr. Li have shouted at you?

例 3：他心情一好,便什麼都好。
  When he is in a good humor, he finds everything agreeable.

例 4：你越是覺得沒問題,就越是有問題。
  Problems will always occur when they are least expected.

例 5：應聘人員,應該擇優錄取,不應該靠關係。
  Selections of employees should be made on a competitive basis, not on connections.

例 6：房間里放三張床擠了一點吧?
  · With three beds, the room will be very cramped, won't it?

· Do you think the room is a bit too small for three beds?

例 7： 人和動物不一樣，人能說話，動物不能。

One of the differences between humans and animals is that humans are capable of speech, but animals are not.

四、改從句為主語

有的漢語句子的主語好像有兩個或多個，甚至像是由兩句話組成的，這就給譯者造成了更大的困難，需要譯者更加細心的分析，才能譯出符合英語的講話習慣和語法規範的句子。例如：

例 1： 這個電影明星離婚了，成了網上的頭條新聞。

The divorce of the famous movie star made the big news on the Internet.

例 2： 總工程師拒絕辭職，全廠工人就罷了工。

The chief engineer's refusal to resign touched off a general strike in the factory.

例 3： 要是再拖延下去就會造成更大的損失。

Any more delay will cause even heavier losses.

例 4： 這個人虛心好學，受到人們的尊敬。

He is respected for his open-mindedness and eagerness to learn.

例 5： 北京成功舉辦 2008 年奧運會，受到國際社會的贊揚。

The success of the 2008 Olympic Games held in Beijing has won the acclaim of the international community.

例 6： 突然刮起了一陣風，把路邊的廣告牌給吹倒了。

A sudden gust of wind blew the billboard down.

由於中國人講話時習慣使用動詞，所以以上五個例句的前半句都像是在陳述動作，如果將其譯成完整的句子，英語譯文讀者就會找不到重點信息，或感到句子拖沓。以例 5 為例,如果將其譯成 The Chinese held the 2008 Beijing Olympic Games successfully and Beijing has won the acclaim of the international community. 這種譯法會讓讀者找不到中心意思。因此在翻譯這五句話時,必須把整個前半句話定為主語,而且必須將其改為名詞形式,這樣後半句話的翻譯就能“水到渠成”了。

五、以重要信息為主語

由於操中英兩種語言的人對“什麼是重點信息”和“如何對待重點信息”的看法或思維方式不同,講話習慣也會不同。例如:

例 1: 他的腿部受了傷。

He was wounded in the leg.

例 2: 襯衣的袖子破了。

The shirt is torn at the sleeves.

例 3: 這些樓房的建築風格不一樣。

These buildings are different from each other in architectural style.

例 4: 我的數學老是不行。

I'm always week in mathematics.

例 5: 這匹馬的左眼睛是瞎的。

The horse is blind in the left eye.

在翻譯這五句話時,必須首先考慮到西方人最關心的重點信息是什麼,再確定什麼是主語。他們習慣首先陳述人或事物的總體狀況,細節次之。翻譯這幾句話時好像是在依次回答這樣幾個問題:

What happened to him?

What's wrong with the shirt?

In what way are these buildings different?

In what aspect are you weak?

In which eye is the horse blind?

六、採用形式主語

如果一個句子的動詞所表示的是主題,即句子所陳述的主要事情,那麼就必須使用英語所特有的句型,即由形式主語It引導的句型,例如:

例1：問題不能這樣看嘛。

It's not right to look at the matter this way.

例2：工人花了兩年時間才把樓建好。

It took the workers as long as two years to put up the building.

例3：有耐心是有好處的。

It pays to be patient.

例4：郵局從這兒幾分鐘就能走到。

It will only take a few minutes to get to the post office from here.

例5：干這活兒二十個人可不夠。

It will take more than 20 people to do the work.

例6：學這一行得經過長期訓練。

It takes long training to learn this trade.

以上所表述的這六種情況僅僅是句子翻譯中比較典型的困難,在實際翻譯工作中,漢語文章中會出現更為複雜的句式。但是,萬變不離其宗,我們要牢記一條原則:漢譯英時,必須首先考慮到譯文讀者的語言習慣和語法規則,即英語最基本的句型是"主謂賓"結構,確定主語是英語造句的首要任務,只有完成了這個任務,後面的工作才能繼續進行。

思考題

1. 為什麼說漢英翻譯的首要任務是確定主語?
2. 為什麼在漢英翻譯中主語有時很難確定?

第七章　連動式的處理

英語詞類豐富,並有形態變化,句子結構嚴謹。主干結構為"主謂句式",一個句子一般只有一個謂語,其功能是為主語服務,表明主語的性質或作用,傳達全句的主要信息。除了謂語動詞外,英語還有連詞、介詞、關係代詞、關係副詞、非謂語動詞等,可以構成無數表示動作的短語。

漢語則是詞類分工不十分明確的無形態變化的語言(immutable language),一切以信息傳遞和意思表達為主,詞序以時間順序和事理順序排列,無關係代詞和關係副詞,連詞和介詞的使用非常有限。但漢語動詞豐富,使用頻繁,一個句子有時連續出現兩個或多個動詞,即連動式(陳宏薇,1998:177-180)。這就給漢英翻譯造成了困難。如果把漢語中的動詞原封不動地再現於英語句子中,讀者就會分不清主次,甚至看不懂原句所要表達的意思。例如:

(1) 我得**去**銀行**貸**款**供**我女兒**上**大學。

(2) 老師**冒著**大雨**上**教室給學生**輔導**去了。

在翻譯這些連動式句子時,要確定主要的動詞,即謂語動詞。只有謂語動詞具有傳遞主語主要信息的功能,其他動詞則處於輔助的次要位置,要用不定式、分詞、介詞、名詞等譯出。以上兩個例句中的主要動詞分別是"**貸款**"和"**上教室**"。其他動詞則按具體情況具體處理。這兩句話可分別譯為:

(1) I must ***ask for*** a bank loan for my daughter's higher education.

(2) The teacher ***went*** to the classroom in the heavy rain to tutor her students.

這種譯法是由中英兩種語言各自的特點決定的,漢語句子不用形態變化來表達語法關係,只能按照表意的需要排列詞序,一般要通過借助詞語、安排詞序或其他辦法分別表達語法意義。一般句子都比較短,常用"竹竿形"分句或按"時間流水"的詞序來逐層敘述思維的各個過程。

英語的特徵是運用形態變化來表達語法關係。句中的詞語或分句之間用語言形式手段(如關聯詞、介詞短語)連接起來,表達語法意義和邏輯關係。現代英語的形態變化主要是動詞的變化和名詞、代詞、形容詞、副詞的變化以及各種詞綴變化。句子一般比較長,但是,由於使用了這些語言形式手段,再長的句子也能分清主次和因果關係,就像"葡萄藤"似的,很容易抓住主干。在漢譯英時,必須採取"化零為整"的方法,以避免語言的拖沓和松散,使譯文嚴謹、簡潔、緊湊,符合英文的表達習慣。下面具體分析幾種比較典型的情況。

一、使用介詞

大量使用介詞或介詞短語是英語的一大特點,例如:林肯的名言 A government **of** the people, **by** the people, **for** the people, shall never perish from the earth. 譯成漢語是"民**有**、民**治**、民**享**之政府永世長存。"此句中的介詞只能以動詞的形式再現於漢語譯文。在漢英翻譯中,漢語動詞經常轉換成英語介詞或介詞短語,下面的例句可稱佳譯:

雪片愈**落**愈多,白茫茫地布滿在天空中,向四處**落**下,**落**在傘上,**落**在轎頂上,**落**在轎夫的笠上,**落**在行人的臉上。　　　　　　　　　　　　(巴金:《家》)

The snowfall was becoming heavier. Snow filled the sky, falling everywhere—**on** umbrellas, **on** the sedan-chairs, **on** the reed caps of the chair carriers, **on** the faces of the pedestrians.　　　　　　　　　　　　　　　　(S. Shapiro　譯)

【分析】原句中四次重複出現的動詞"落"被英語介詞 on 代替,既符合英語語言習慣,又保持了漢語原文的韻律美。

請看以下例句:
例1:他**穿著**大衣就**跳進**了河里**去救落水**的孩子。

He jumped into the river **with** his overcoat **on** to rescue the drowning child.

【分析】漢語原句的主要動作是"跳進了河里","穿著大衣"是"跳河"時的狀態;"去救落水的孩子"則是"跳河"的目的。在英語譯文中用介詞 with … on 和動詞不定式 to rescue 即可。

例2:**坐過牢的人**比**沒坐過牢的人**找工作難。

It's more difficult for a person **with** a prison record to find a job than those **without** such a record.

【分析】"坐牢"這層意思在英語中不必用動詞來表達, 用介詞短語 with a prison record 更合適。

例3：他**走了**三個鐘頭的路, 不知不覺**到了**一個村子, 一個人也**沒有**, 只**有**幾條沒有主人的狗。

After three-hour walk, he ***found himself in*** a deserted village, with a few stray dogs in it.

【分析】原句的主要意思是"不知不覺到了一個村子", 這層意思, 用動詞短語 found himself in a village 來表達即可, 其他動詞"走了、沒有人、只有"要用介詞 after, with 和過去分詞 deserted 譯出。

例4：大廳的牆上**掛著**三十幾幅油畫, 都**是**大師的手筆, 大廳**看起來**就是小小的美術館。

With over 30 oils, all by old masters, the hall ***looks like*** a small gallery.

【分析】原句中的主要信息是"大廳看起來就是小小的美術館", 必須用動詞表示, 其他動詞"掛著、都是"可用介詞 with, by 來表達。以下例句同理, 不做詳細分析。

例5：我看見一個人肩膀**很寬**, 用一只手就把杠鈴**舉起來了**。

I saw a man ***with*** broad shoulders lifting the barbell ***with*** only one hand.

例6：用中國的標準來**衡量**, 他的身材算是高的了。

He is quite tall ***by*** Chinese standards.

例7：這個城市**變化很大**, 已經認不出來了。

The city can hardly be recognized ***because of*** the great changes that have taken place there.

例8：鷄蛋賣七塊錢一公斤, 比上個月**便宜**了兩毛。

Eggs are seven yuan a kilo, ***down by*** 20 cents from last month.

例9：他給抓起來了, 罪名**是**盜竊。

He was arrested ***on*** a charge of theft.

例 10：鈴聲**一響**，觀眾回到看臺，**接著看**下半場的比賽。

At the bell, the spectators began to return to the stands **for** the second half of the game.

二、使用分詞

　　有時漢語中的非謂語動詞所表達意思的複雜程度超出了介詞短語所具有的功能，我們就要借助於現在分詞或過去分詞了。下面我們分析一下分詞的各種作用。

　　1. 表示伴隨動作

例 1：他哀傷地站在船上，不停地**轉過頭**去，**望著**漸漸**遠去**的山峰。

He stood sadly on the deck of the ship, **keeping on looking** over his shoulder at the gradually **receding** mountains.

例 2：船順流而下，像箭一樣疾駛前進，這**使我想起**了李白的那首名詩。

The boat went downstream swiftly like a flying arrow, **reminding** me of the famous poem by Li Bai, the most famous poet of the Tang Dynasty.

例 3：體育館里衝出來一大群人，**又喊又笑**，有的趕公交車，有的叫出租。

A large crowd of people rushed out of the stadium **shouting** and **laughing** to catch buses or to call taxis.

例 4：他**走了**進來，**步上**講臺，開始講課。

Coming into the room and **stepping onto** the stage, he began to give his lecture.

例 5：他坐在那兒，一邊**看**相片兒，一邊**掉眼淚**。

He sat there **looking at** the pictures in tears.

例 6：他**擠著上車**，手機被人偷了。

Squeezing his way onto the bus, he had his mobile phone stolen.

例 7：他站在倒塌的房子面前，**束手無策**。

He stood before a collapsed house, **not knowing** what to do.

例 8：老人拿起電話，**不知道**能不能找到他女兒。

The old man picked up the receiver, *wondering* whether he could reach his daughter.

例 9：他**冒著**風暴爬上了山頂。

Braving the storm, he worked his way up to the top of the mountain.

例 10：他講了十五分鐘的話，強烈譴責這次恐怖襲擊事件。

He spoke for 15 minutes, *denouncing* the terrorist attack.

例 11：他站在桌子旁邊，仔細**研究著**桌面的光潔度。

He stood by the table, *examining* carefully the polish of its top.

例 12：他活兒只干了一半就**丟下**鏟子走了。

Throwing away his shovel, he quit *leaving* his work only half done.

例 13：他又叫又鬧，非**要**離開醫院不可。

He made a scene, *demanding* to be released from the hospital.

2. 表示結果

例 1：他從自行車上摔下來，把腿**摔壞**了。

He fell from his bicycle, *breaking* his leg.

例 2：洪水呼嘯而過，**淹沒**了許多村莊。

The floodwaters rampaged along, *submerging* many villages in their path.

例 3：警察向劫匪開了一槍，**打傷**了他的左腿。

The policeman shot at the robber, *wounding* him in the left leg.

例 4：颶風襲擊了沿海的一些城市，**造成**了嚴重的財產損失。

The hurricane struck some cities along the coast, *causing* heavy property losses.

3. 用分詞短語 Having（Being）＋ participle 表示原因

例 1：這所學校全國聞名，吸引了很多學生。

— 61 —

Being a very famous school throughout the country，it attracts a lot of students.

例 2：他樂於助人，在班上人緣很好。

Being always ready to help others，he is very popular in his class.

例 3：他太愛吹牛，在班里很沒人緣兒。

Being boastful all the time，he is not popular at all with his classmates.

例 4：這個人生下來就是盲人，他一時也離不開人的照顧。

Being born blind，he is always in need of help.

例 5：他把工作做完了以後，就離開了辦公室。

Having finished his work，he left his office.

例 6：他在這個城市里住了一輩子，對這個城市了如指掌。

Having lived in this city all his life，he knows the city like the back of his hand.

例 7：他一口氣唱了三個鐘頭，把嗓子都唱啞了。

Having sung for three hours non-stop，he lost his voice.

例 8：他經歷過多次戰爭，什麼苦都能吃。

Having lived through many wars，this person can endure all kinds of hardship.

　　以上列舉了這麼多分類清晰的例句，主要是為了便於分析漢語連動式英譯的幾種典型情況，以便引起初學翻譯的人的注意，在漢譯英時要避免詞與詞的對譯。其實，翻譯實踐中出現的實際情況肯定會比以上所舉的例子複雜得多，關鍵是我們必須善於識別，酌情處理，使譯文更加符合英語讀者的表達習慣和語法規則。

思考題

1. 漢英語言句子結構的主要差異體現在哪些方面？
2. 確定了謂語動詞以後，為什麼漢語中的其他動詞不能以動詞形式再現於英語句子中？

第八章　從屬信息的翻譯

　　翻譯的基本單位（unit）既不是詞，也不是句子，而是"信息層次"或"意群"。一個句子至少要有一個意群，也就是一層意思，句子一般都是由多層次意群組成的，層次越多越不容易分析處理，翻譯起來就更難。句子翻譯的一個重要環節是謂語的確定，明確了謂語動詞的位置就等於建起了句子的主干，因為只有謂語動詞具有傳遞主要信息的功能，其他動詞則處於輔助的次要位置。由於漢語的流水句、散碎句很多，意群界線不分明，識別難度更大。但在英語中，從屬信息必須用語法手段明確地表示出來。例如：

例 1：

　　我兒子正上學呢。

　　My son | goes to school | . （一層意思）

　　我兒子每天七點去上學。

　　My son | goes to school | at seven o'clock every day | . （兩層意思）

　　我兒子每天七點騎車去上學。

　　My son | goes to school | by bike | at seven o'clock every day | . （三層意思）

　　我兒子每天七點騎車去上學，風雨無阻。

　　My son | goes to school | by bike | at seven o'clock every day | , | rain or shine | . （四層意思）

例 2：

我打了他。	I hit him.	（主要信息）
我狠狠打了他。	I hit him *hard.*	（程度）
我照他臉上狠狠打了他。	I hit him *hard in the face.*	（程度、方式）

我拿棍子打了他。	I hit him *with a rod.*	（方式）
我把他打流血了。	I hit him *until he bled.*	（程度）
我把他打得流了好多血。	I hit him *so hard that he bled profusely.*	（程度）
他罵我，我才打了他。	I hit him *because he insulted me.*	（原因）

在例 2 中，"我打了他"是主要信息，其他成分都是從屬信息，表明或修飾與中心意思相關的信息或狀態。

在很多情況下，判斷信息的主次要靠上下文和譯者對原文的理解，例如，翻譯這個句子：**鳥兒栖樹，歡鳴不已**。起碼有四個譯文：

（1）The birds are *sitting* in the trees and are *chirping* happily. （**栖樹**和**歡鳴**同等重要）

（2）The birds are *sitting* in the trees chirping happily. （**栖樹**比**歡鳴**重要）

（3）The birds in the trees are *chirping* happily. （**歡鳴**比**栖樹**重要）

（4）*Happily* the birds are chirping in the trees. （這句話的重點是鳥兒的"**歡快**"狀態）

以上例句所包含的信息較為單一，比較容易判斷。包含多層次信息的句子就很難分析、判斷。請看下列例句：

例 1：**有一個人**打著手電筒，沿街**向我走來**，街上闃無一人，只有幾只貓在找吃的。

With a torch（flashlight）in hand, *a man was walking towards me* along the street which was utterly deserted except for a few cats looking for food.

例 2：**那年經濟情況不錯**，國家收入增加了 2%，失業率降到了 5%，是十年來最低的。

It was a good year for the economy with 2% increase in government revenue and a mere 5% of unemployment rate, the lowest in 10 years.

例 3：那個時候，**戲劇界的形勢非常嚴重**，戲劇節目貧乏，上座率低，劇場經營困難，演員生活無法保證。

The performing arts industry was beset with serious problems, such as a shrinking repertoire, poor box office draw, theatre struggling for survival, unstable incomes for actors.

【分析】例 1 中的"有一個人向我走來"，例 2 中的"那年經濟情況不錯"，例 3 中的"戲劇界的形勢非常嚴重"是主要信息，其他信息分別是環境描述（例 1）或說明主要信息的例證(例 2 和例 3)。

　　如果詳細分析，英語句子中的非主要信息一般按照實際情況和交際的需要，使用同位語、分詞、定語從句和獨立結構的方式來表示不同於主要謂語的從屬地位。下面我們分別進行分析。

一、同位語(appositive)

　　同位語，顧名思義，就是具有同等意義和語法功能的詞或短語。完全等同的同謂語在漢語中比較容易識別，例如：

例1：**喬治·布什**，美國上一任總統，1975 年就隨他父親住在北京。

George Bush, ***former US President***, was living in Beijing with his father in 1975.

例2：魯迅，**紹興人，**是中國新文學運動的創始人之一。

Lu Xun, ***a native of Shaoxing***, was one of the founders of the Chinese New Literary Movement.

　　在很多情況下，漢語中的某些從屬信息用"是"字來表示，這個"是"與英語中的表語動詞 to be 不同，其語法功能只是表明"是"字前後的詞具有等同或部分等同意義，也可稱為部分同位語 (partial appositive)。例如：

例3：漢白玉**是**出產在北京的一種大理石，是建築紀念碑的好材料。

Hanbaiyu, ***a kind of marble produced in Beijing***, is a good material for monuments.

例4：老王真**是**個好人，鄰居們都喜歡他，可惜上禮拜搬走了。

Mr. Wang, ***a nice man***, loved by all his neighbors, moved away last week.

例5：私人汽車 20 年前還**是**奢侈品，如今在中國大城市里已經不稀奇了。

Private cars, ***a luxury only 20 years ago***, are a common sight in the big cities of China.

例6：李教授**是**個老北京人，卻對北京不太了解。

Professor Li, ***a native of Beijing***, ironically knows very little about the city.

例7：李先生，就**是**你昨天在機場見到的那個中年人，又回美國了。

Mr. Li, ***the middle-aged man you met at the airport yesterday***, has returned to

America.

例8：大白菜過去是北京人冬天的看家菜,現在一年四季都能買到。

Bok choy or Chinese cabbage, ***the main winter vegetable for Beijingers in the past***, can be bought the whole year round.

例9：手機在 20 年前還是社會地位的象徵,現在幾乎都成災了。

Mobile phones, ***a status symbol*** 20 ***years ago***, are ubiquitous nowadays.

例10：蔡元培是一位知名教育家,在北京大學初期曾做過一任校長。

Mr. Cai Yuanpei, ***a renowned educator***, served one term as the president of Peking University in its early days.

二、介詞(preposition)與分詞(participle)

在沒有必要表明時間概念的情況下,使用介詞或分詞短語比較適宜。

例1：**你太鬧了**,我沒法工作。(表示原因)

With you making so much noise, I can't work here.

例2：**還有三天就必須完工了**,他們正在日夜不停地趕工。(表示原因)

With only three days left to the deadline of the project, they are speeding up day and night.

例3：有個人**穿著一身黑**,夜里偷偷地進了學校,很快被發現,帶到了辦公室進行詢問。(表示狀態)

A man ***in black*** stole into the school and was soon discovered and taken to the office to be questioned.

例4：美國總統**四年選舉一次**,這讓想連任的總統過多地花費精力。(表示情況)

The US presidential election, ***held in every four years***, costs the presidents who want to be re-elected too much energy.

例5：這些機器**才從國外買來**,還沒有在廠里裝配上。(表示狀態)

These machines, ***brought in from abroad only recently***, have not been installed in the factory.

例 6：大火造成了嚴重的財產損失,估計有 200 萬美元。(表示原因)
The property ***lost in the big fire*** is estimated at two million US dollars.

例 7：這個求職的人,**三次面試都沒通過,**他不想再試第四次了。(表示原因)
This applicant, ***disqualified in all the three interviews***, would give up trying a fourth time.

例 8：洪水汹涌澎湃,所到之處,**萬物俱毀。**(表示結果)
The floodwaters rampaged along, ***destroying everything in their path.***

例 9：這家商店**問題太多,**只好關門。(表示原因)
Beset with too many problems, this store has to close down.

例 10：他把門**砰地一關,**怒氣衝衝地走出了房間。(表示方式)
　Slamming the door shut angrily, he walked out of the room.
　He walked out of the room angrily, ***shutting the door with a bang.***

三、定語從句 (attributive clause)

　　如果需要說明時間概念或有必要進一步表示與主語相關的信息,就必須用定語從句。漢語中的"的"字結構是最明顯的標記。

例 1：你來的路上見到**的**那家賓館有百年歷史了。
The hotel ***you saw*** on your way here is 100 years old.

例 2：到過北京**的**人都知道頤和園在哪里。
Those ***who have visited Beijing*** know where the Summer Palace is.

例 3：坐在臺上的那個人就是演了一部電影就成名**的**演員嗎?
Is that the man ***sitting on the stage*** the actor ***who became famous overnight after making only one movie***?

例 4： 因為偷自行車讓警察抓走**的**那個人是我家鄰居。

The person **who has been arrested on the charge of steeling bicycles** is my neighbor.

例 5： 1945 年結束**的**第二次世界大戰，在人類歷史上是空前殘酷的。

World War II , **which ended in 1945** , is the bloodiest war in history.

例 6： 三年以前歇業**的**那家商店昨天又恢復營業了。

This store , **which closed down three years ago** , reopened yesterday.

　　沒有"的"字結構的句子給我們判斷信息的主次帶來了一定的難度，但一般來講，漢語習慣於把條件放在句前，結果放後，重要的事後說。

例 7： **去年我們種了**幾十棵樹，一半沒活。

Half of the dozens of trees **we planted last year** did not survive.

例 8： **上星期我從圖書館借了**本書，丟了。

The book **I borrowed from the library** last week has been lost.

例 9： **明朝是被一次農民革命給推翻的**，那次農民革命後來失敗了。

The peasant revolution **that overthrew the Ming Dynasty** met its Waterloo afterwards.

例 10： 有一個朋友，**你不認識**，曾經向我打聽你的情況。

A friend of mine , **whom you don't know** , once asked me about you.

例 11： **來北京開會的人昨天到達**，他們都住在北京飯店。

Those **who arrived in Beijing yesterday to attend the conference** are staying in Beijing Hotel.

例 12： 1976 年唐山市**毀於地震**，在 30 年中已經發展成為現代化的工業城。

Tangshan City , **which was devastated by an earthquake** in 1976 , was built into a modern industrial city in only 30 years.

例 13： **他認識一個朋友**，住在美國，每周給他發短信。

A friend of his **who lives in America** texts him every week.

例 14：他開的車**是二手貨**，常在路上拋錨，很麻煩。

The car **he bought second-hand** causes him a lot of trouble as it often breaks down on the road.

例 15：很多人**為希望工程捐款**，我想給他們每人寫封感謝信。

I want to write a letter of thanks to each of those **who have donated money** to the Hope Project.

例 16：這個演員十年前**得過最佳男演員獎**，已經有三四年沒拍過片子了。

The actor, **who won the Best Actor Award** ten years ago, hasn't made any movies for the last three or four years.

例 17：這位朋友 40 年前**移居澳大利亞**，**去了很多地方**，知道那里的一些情況。

This friend of mine, **who emigrated to Australia** 40 years ago and **has traveled extensively** there, is well informed about the country.

還有一種情況必須用定語從句：一句話由兩部分或兩個分句組成，一個分句是陳述事實，另一個是講話人的評論。評論部分要用 **which** 引導的從句，表示這是講話人的看法。例如：

例 18：他罵了裁判，**這是不行的**。

He swore at the referee, **which** is not allowed.

例 19：他升職了，我覺得**他受之無愧**。

He has been promoted, **which** I think is what he deserves.

例 20：他承認了錯誤，**真沒想到**。

He admitted to his mistakes（He said he was wrong）, **which** is unexpected.

例 21：他為地震災區捐了一筆錢，**這很慷慨**，事後他又後悔了，**這就很可笑了**。

He donated a sum of money for the earthquake-stricken area, **which** was very generous of him, but he regretted it afterwards, **which** is rather ridiculous.

例 22：他用 11 秒跑了一百米，這對沒受過訓練的人來說**很不容易**。

His record for the 100-meter dash is 11 seconds, **which** is extraordinary to an amateur.

例 23：他辭去了做了十年的工作，**這是他一生中做的最大的一件錯事**。

He resigned from the job he had been doing for ten years, *which* is the biggest mistake he made in his life.

例 24：正在上課，他沒道歉就進來，走到座位上去了，**這是不允許的**。

He came into the classroom and walked to his seat without apologizing when the class was in session, *which* is not allowed.

四、獨立結構（absolute structure）

如果在一句話中出現了兩個主語或施動者，就必須判斷哪一個在整體意義上更為重要，哪一個屬於從屬地位，較為次要的角色就由獨立結構來表示。獨立結構是沒有謂語動詞的從句。比較下列兩組句子：

例 1：A. 運動員隨著音樂列隊入場。（單主語）

Marching to the music, the athletes filed into the arena. （分詞）

　　　B. 運動員列隊入場，**最前邊的一個舉著國旗**。（雙主語）

The athletes filed into the arena, *the one walking in the front holding the national flag.* （獨立結構）

例 2：A. 他慢慢地往烟囱上爬，不知道能不能爬到頂。（單主語）

He worked his way up the chimney slowly, *wondering if he could reach the top.* （分詞）

　　　B. 他慢慢地往烟囱上爬，**兩腿發顫，兩手緊緊抓著梯子**。（多主語）

He worked his way up the chimney slowly, *his legs trembling* and *his hands gripping the ladder.* （獨立結構）

請看下列例句：

例 3：冷風中立著幾棵樹，**樹葉都掉光了**。

A few trees stood in the cold wind, *their leaves all gone.*

例 4：他躺在床上，**腦袋埋在枕頭里**。

He was lying in bed, *his head buried in the pillow.*

例 5：他**兩腿發抖**,慢慢走上臺階。

He walked up the steps slowly, *his legs trembling.*

例 6：他看了兩個小時的書,**興致越來越濃。**

He was reading for two hours, *his interest growing.*

例 7：路的盡頭是座空房子,**門窗都沒有了。**

An empty house stands at the end of the road, *the door and windows all gone.*

例 8：他坐在地上喘著氣,**帽子一直拉著,把臉遮了一半。**

He sat on the ground gasping, *his cap pulled half way down his face.*

例 9：他敞著懷,露出**結實的胸膛**,用斧子在劈木柴。

He is chopping firewood with an axe, *his deep chest showing* through his unbuttoned shirt.

例 10：冠軍隊坐在接待室里,有說有笑,**眼里閃著喜悅,聲調里充滿自豪。**

The champion team sat in the reception room, talking and laughing, *their eyes filled with delights and their voices with pride.*

值得注意的是,以上以分門別類的方式說明四種情況只是為了便於論述,在實際翻譯工作中,並不存在絕對的判斷標準或表達方式。信息的主從地位除了要靠事件的前因後果,或是主要動作還是伴隨動作來判斷以外,在理解原文時,還有一個語感問題,也就是譯者的實際經驗和邏輯知識。這就需要譯者平時善於觀察漢英語言的差異,在讀書時善於分析聯想,才能摸索出規律來。

思考題

1. 在漢英翻譯中為什麼有必要判斷信息的主從地位? 是否可以按照漢語的表達順序直譯成英語?
2. 除了句子的語法結構,判斷信息的主次還有哪些依據?

第九章　虛擬語氣的翻譯

　　在漢英翻譯中,感情色彩越濃的語言,翻譯難度越大,如把表示希望、假設、猜測、埋怨等虛擬語氣轉換成英語,既是一個判斷理解過程,又是一個結構轉換過程。其原因仍然是漢英兩種語言在表達思想感情方面,存在較大的差異。漢語表達很多情感主要靠語氣的變化、聲調的升降和感嘆詞的運用來完成,而英語則運用語法手段,也就是結構變化來表示。請看以下對比:

事實陳述	虛擬語氣
今天不是星期六,我還得早起。 It's not Saturday today, I have to get up early.	**假如**今天是星期六,我就不必早起了。 If it *were* Saturday, I *wouldn't* get up early.
我已經不年輕了,不能考博了。 I'm not young, so I can't apply for a study of Ph. D.	**如果**我年輕十歲,我也**會**考博的。 If I *were* ten years younger, I *would* also study for a Ph. D.
我不會講法語。 I don't speak French.	我**要是**會講法語**就好了**。 *If only I could* speak French!

　　在漢語中,"假如"、"如果"、"要是"都是虛擬語氣的明顯的篇章標記(discourse markers),比較容易識別。但是,在實際生活中,中國人是不用這些標記的,這就給英譯增加了難度。例如:

例1:明天你來,咱就一塊兒去看電影;**你不來**,我可就自己去了。

　　　If you come here tomorrow, we*'ll* go to see a movie, or I*'ll* go myself.

例 2：他考試**要是**不及格，我一點都不奇怪。上次考試不難，他就不及格，可是那些題目比他低一個年級的同學都能做出來。他現在有些擔心，我理解，**要是**我也會擔心的。

I *would* not be surprised if he *fails* in the next examination, because he *failed* in the last one, which *was* so easy that even students of the lower grade *could have made it.* He is quite worried now. I *would* feel the same way.

一、would 的功能和用法

在漢語日常對話中，最常用的虛擬語氣的標記是"要是(如果)……就會"，英語中相對應的詞是"if...would"。請看例句：

例 1：**要是**我才十幾歲的話，我也**會**同我的父母住在一起的。
If I were a teenager, I *would* also be living with my parents.

例 2：**要是**我下周日不這麼忙的話，我**會**同你們聚聚的。
If I were not that busy next Sunday, I *would* join you in a party.

例 3：**要不是**這麼晚的話，我就出去散步了。
If it were not this late, *I would* be out taking a walk.

例 4：**要是**我考試及格的話，我現在就是研究生了。
If I had passed the examinations, *I would* be a post-graduate student now.

例 5：**要是**我們組織一次羽毛球比賽，班上誰**會**得冠軍？
If we organize a badminton competition, who *would* be the champion?

例 6：**如果**你教外國人中文，從哪兒開始？是會話還是閱讀？
If you teach foreigners Chinese, from where *would* you begin? From reading or speaking?

例 7：**如果**發生第三次世界大戰，**會**用原子彈嗎？
In a third world war, *would* nuclear weapons be used?

例 8：在北京,這類房子的房租是三百塊錢一個月,**要是**在廣州應該是多少?

The rent of this kind of house is 300 yuan RMB a month in Beijing. How much **would** that be in Guangzhou?

漢語經常省略"要是(如果)……就會",但是英語中的 would 不能用其他時態來代替. 例如:

例 9：這雙鞋折合美金多少錢?

How much **would** the pair of shoes be in US dollars?

例 10：在北京我們穿得很多,在廣州就沒有必要了。

Such warm clothes we wear in Beijing **would** not be necessary in Guangzhou.

例 11：這種房子太通風了,在北方就行不通。

The house **would** be too airy for comfort in north China.

例 12：你沒叫我十點鐘來呀,否則我是不會遲到的。

You didn't ask me to come at ten o'clock. Otherwise I **wouldn't** be late.

例 13：這樣的事我是不會干的,這太可笑了。

I **wouldn't** do anything like that; it's ridiculous.

例 14：你這句話里的這個詞,英國人是不會用的。

An English writer **would** not use the word you used in this sentence.

例 15：他現在的工資是一個月 2000 元人民幣,生活很不錯;在美國這點兒錢只夠他一個人吃飯的,還有點兒勉強。

He is comfortably off with a monthly salary of 2000 RMB here in China, but the same amount of money **would** barely enough cover his food expenses in America.

在對過去已經發生的情況進行假設時,英譯文中要用 would have done 來表示,例如:

例 16： 你昨天為什麼沒來? 你要是來了,就一定會碰到我兒子了。

Why didn't you come yesterday? Otherwise, you *would have seen* my son.

例 17： 去上海的航班取消了,要不我早就動身了。

The flight to Shanghai has been canceled, or, I *would have set* off a long time ago.

例 18： 他一口氣工作了 12 個小時,你會這樣干嗎?

He worked for 12 hours without a break. *Would* you *have done* anything like that?

例 19： 他跳進冰窟窿里把孩子救了出來,你會這樣嗎?

He jumped into the iced-up river to rescue a drowning child, *would* you *have done* that?

例 20： 他對這事大動肝火,很正常,換了誰都會這樣。

He went to the roof at the matter, which is understandable. Anyone *would have reacted* this way.

例 21： 他這十年騎自行車上下班所走的路,相當於從北京到莫斯科走了一趟。

The bicycle-trips he made from home to the workplace and back in the last ten years *would have taken* him from Beijing to Moscow.

　　如果假設的情況發生的可能性更小的話,要用 *could* 來代替 *would*。

例 22： 有些歷史學家說,1945 年 8 月的那兩顆原子彈結束了太平洋戰爭,否則,日本還能打上半年。你說呢?

Some historians insist that the two atomic bombs dropped over Japan ended the Pacific War, or Japan *could have held on* for another half a year. What's your comment?

例 23： 現在中國在經濟上所取得的成就在 20 年前是不可想象的。

The economic achievements China has accomplished now *could not have been imagined* 20 years ago.

二、would 與 will 的用法和區別

人們在預測未來情況時,有時認為事情很有可能發生,語氣較為肯定,在英譯時,要用 will,如果認為事情不會發生,純屬假設,或對已經發生的事進行假設,仍然要用 would。請比較下列幾組句子:

例 1: 明天肯定還這麼冷。Tomorrow it *will* be just as cold, if not colder. (語氣肯定)

明天還會這麼冷。Tomorrow it *would* be just as cold. (不太肯定)

例 2: 你要是聽醫生的話,你的病情就不會惡化。

· If you follow the doctor's advice, your conditions *will* not get worse. (病情穩定)

· If you had followed the doctor's advice, your conditions *would* not be this bad.

(病情不佳)

例 3: 如果我說過這句話,我就得道歉。

· If I *said* anything like that, *I'll* apologize. (記不清說沒說過這句話)

· If I *had said* anything like that, I *would* apologize. (肯定沒說過這句話)

例 4: 這個活兒換了別人,30 天是干不完的。

· Others *will* never finish the job in 30 days. (在干活之前說這句話)

· Others *would have never finished* it in 30 days. (在干活之後說這句話)

例 5: 一個大國如果不節制生育,就會出現人口問題。

If a country with a large population does not promote family planning, there *will* be bad population problems. (肯定會發生的一般假設)

如果我國在 40 年前就實行"只生一個"的政策,我們的人口問題就不會這樣嚴峻。

If we *had adopted* the "one-child-family policy" 40 years ago, China's population problem *would not be* so serious today. (對過去未發生的事情的假設)

例 6：如果美國轟炸伊朗的核設施,結果會怎麼樣?

If the US *bombs* the Iran's nuclear facilities, what *will* happen?（很有可能發生）

If the US *bombed* the Iran's nuclear facilities, what *would* happen?（沒有可能發生）

三、should 的功能和用法

1. 提醒該做的事（To show unfulfilled expectations）

例 1：—你知道 BISU 指什麼嗎?　　　　Do you know what "BISU" stands for?

—不知道。　　　　　　　　　　Sorry, I don't know.

—你應該知道。　　　　　　　　Well, you *should*.

例 2：—你申請了那份工作嗎?　　　　Did you apply for the job?

—還沒呢。　　　　　　　　　　Not yet.

—應該申請了。　　　　　　　　You *should have.*

例 3：我當初真應該買房子,現在後悔也晚了。

I *should have bought* a house. It's too late now.（對該做卻沒做的事表示後悔）

2. 表示埋怨或輕微的批評（To show mild criticism）

漢語中的語氣詞"嘛"就是表示埋怨或輕微批評的標記,請看下例:

例 1：這兒應該有個名字**嘛**。

There *should* be a name here.

例 2：牆上該掛幾幅畫**嘛**。

There *should* be some pictures on the wall.

例 3：你應該早點兒來**嘛**。

You *should have been* here earlier.

例 4：你應該早點兒告訴我**嘛**。

You *should have told* me earlier.

例 5：這家旅館的前廳怎麼沒有椅子？至少也得有四五把**嘛**。

Why! There are no chairs in the lobby! There *should* be four or five of them at least.

有時在沒有"嘛"字的情況下，就得看是否有"應該"一詞來判斷埋怨的語氣：

例 6：辦公室里**不應該**有床。

There *shouldn't* be a bed in the office.

例 7：你**不應該**把車停在這兒。

You *shouldn't* park the car here.

例 8：他**不應該**這麼自傲。

He *shouldn't* be so arrogant.

例 9：你**真應該**小心點兒。

You *should have been* more careful.

例 10：他真**不應該**打裁判。

He *shouldn't have hit* the referee.

例 11：所有的學生都**應該**在規定的時間內交論文，可有些人就是不聽。

All students *should* submit their theses by a given date, but some of them don't!

例 12：他**不應該**這麼沒耐心。

He *shouldn't* be so impatient.

例 13：這個標點符號**應該**放在中間，**不應該**放在句尾。

The punctuation mark *should* be in the middle of the sentence, not at the end of it.

同 should 的用法相近的表達法 had better do 可以表示語氣強烈的建議(strong recommendation or advisability)。

例 14: 你**應該**麻利點兒,要不就趕不上火車了。

You**'d better** be quick, or you'll miss the train.

例 15: 他**不應該**再犯錯誤了。

He**'d better** not make another mistake.

例 16: 我想我**應該**把門鎖上。

I suppose **I'd better** lock the door.

例 17: 我可別把他們吵醒了。

I'd better not wake them up.

3. 表示猜測 (To show guessing)

例 1: 都 8 點 5 分了,老師**應該**馬上就到。

It's five past eight and the teacher **should** be here soon.

例 2: 你到黃山時,我們**應該**在那兒待了三天了。

When you get to Huangshan Mountain, we **should** be there for three days.

例 3: 這只是個小樂隊,一個吉他手也就夠了。

It's only a small band. One guitarist **should** be enough.

例 4: 這時候他**應該**到天津了。

He **should have arrived** in Tianjin now. (He **should be** in Tianjin now.)

例 5: 如果你想比我們早到這兒,你就**應該**在星期五離開北京。

If you had wanted to get here before us, you **should have left** Beijing on Friday.

例 6: 這活兒花了我三個星期,當初我真應該聽你的,那樣有兩個星期**也就夠了**。

It took me three weeks to do the work. I should have taken your advice. I **would have done** it in only two weeks.

四、should 與 must 的用法和區別

一般來講,must 表示"告誡"、"要求",或語氣比較肯定的猜測,should 則表示"責任",或語氣不太肯定的猜測。

例 1: 全體學生**都要**提前五分鐘到教室。(要求)

All students *must arrive* five minutes before the class begins.

全體學生**都應該**提前五分鐘到教室。(責任)

All students *should arrive* five minutes before the class begins.

例 2: 火車八點鐘開,你**應該**七點鐘從家里走。

The train leaves at 8:00. You *must* leave home at seven. (事前提醒)

火車已經開了,你**應該**七點鐘就從家里走嘛。

The train has left. You *should have left* home at seven. (事後埋怨)

例 3: 那**應該**是 1945 年。

That *must have been* in 1945. (比較肯定)

That *should have been* in 1945. (不太肯定)

例 4: 你**可不要**撒謊。

You *mustn't* lie. (事前告誡)

你**不應該**撒謊嘛。

You *shouldn't have lied.* (事後批評)

例 5: 考卷**要**寫上名字。

All the test papers *must* carry their names. (提醒)

考卷**應該**寫上名字嘛。

The test papers *should* carry their names. (批評)

例 6: 你**可得**告訴我出了什麼事。

You *must tell* me what happens. (事前提醒)

你**應該**告訴我出了什麼事嘛。

You *should have told* me what happened. (事後批評)

例 7： 說英文就應該按英國人的規矩，**不應該**生造。

Speak English the way the English do. Please ***don't*** invent. （事前提醒）

說英文就應該按英國人的規矩，你**不應該**生造嘛。

Speak English the way the English do. You ***shouldn't have invented.*** （事後批評）

例 8： 出了問題你可要**立刻**告訴我，千萬不要隱瞞。

You ***must*** tell me if things go wrong. Don't try to cover it up.

出了問題你**應該**立刻告訴我嘛，怎麼能隱瞞呢？

You ***should have told me*** when things went wrong. How could you have tried to cover it up?

　　需要注意的是，在翻譯書面材料時，沒有語音語調的輔助因素，判斷漢語的虛擬語氣比較難。這就需要譯者通過自己的語感和對漢語交際習慣的掌握，仔細閱讀上下文來判斷講話人的語氣，然後才能在譯文中正確運用相應的表達法。

思考題

1. 英譯虛擬語氣的難點究竟在哪里？是在對漢語原文的理解上還是在英譯文的表達上？
2. 在翻譯虛擬語氣時，有哪些因素需要考慮？

第十章　靜態和動態的翻譯

　　世間萬物有靜態（static）與動態（dynamic）之分，描述這兩種狀態的語言也有區別。描寫情景、狀態的詞是靜態詞，陳述動作、行為的詞是動態詞。漢英語言在表達這兩種狀態方面存在較大差異。最主要的不同點是：漢語無論是敘述動態還是靜態，傾向於多用動詞，輔以"著、了、過、地"等助詞來加以區分，除此之外沒有明顯的時態標記；英語傾向於多用名詞、形容詞和介詞短語來表示靜態，用動詞表示動作，且有明顯的時態標記。因此，在靜態與動態的漢英翻譯時，就有可能出現障礙。判斷漢語句子是動態還是靜態，除了助詞以外，還要靠語感和對句子上下文的理解。請對比下列幾組句子：

例 1：冬天樹葉都**掉光**了。

　　Tree leaves *are all gone* in winter.（靜態）

　　冬天一到，樹葉就**掉**。

　　When winter comes, tree leaves *begin to fall*.（動態）

例 2：機器**壞了**三天了。

　　The machine *is broken* for three days.（靜態）

　　機器什麼時候**壞的**？

　　When did the machine *break down*?（動態）

例 3：市長**任職**五年了。

　　The mayor has been *in office* for five years.（靜態）

　　新市長下月**上任**。

　　The new mayor will *take office* next month.（動態）

例 4：這項工程由我**負責**。

I'm *in charge of* the project. (靜態)

我從去年**開始負責**這項工程。

I *took charge of* the project last year. (動態)

例 5：我**愛**這個城市。

I *love* this city. (靜態)

我一到這兒就**愛上了**這個城市。

I *fell in love* with the city as soon as I came here. (動態)

例 6：他一走進房間就**開燈**。

He *turned on* the lights when he entered the room. (動態)

他回來的時候燈就是**開著**的。

Lights *were on* when he came back. (靜態)

例 7：我見到他時，他**淚流滿面**。

He *was all tears* when I saw him. (靜態)

一見我來看他，他**掉眼淚了**。

He *burst into tears* when I came to see him. (動態)

例 8：房子**正在粉刷**。

The house *is being painted.* (動態)

房子**粉刷得很好**。

The house *is very well painted.* (靜態)

例 9：他上星期**生病了**。

He *got sick* last week. (動態)

他已經**病了**一個星期了。

He *has been sick* for a week. (靜態)

例 10：我兒子**當兵兩年了**。

My son has been *in the army* for two years. (靜態)

我兒子**兩年前當兵了**。

My son *joined the army* two years ago. (動態)

例 11：圖書館禮拜天**開門**嗎?

Does the library *open* on Sundays? (動態)

圖書館 24 小時**開門**。

The library *is open* 24 hours a day. (靜態)

例 12：他**活到**了 90 歲。

He *lived to* 90 years. (動態)

他現在還**活著**嗎?

Is he still *alive*? (靜態)

例 13：他們**來了**。

They *have come.* (動態)

他們**來了**幾小時了。

They'*ve been here* for a few hours. (靜態)

一、英語中表示施事者的名詞(doer)

英語中大量由動詞派生的(如以-er 或-or 結尾的)詞含有行為和動作意義,但仍屬於靜態詞。例如:

例 1：他既**不抽烟**,也**不喝酒**。

He is a *nonsmoker* and a *teetotaler.*

例 2：今天你怎麼老是**看表**等著下班呢!

You're really a *clock-watcher* today.

例 3：他失業以後,就**很不合群**了。

Since he lost his job, he's been a *loner.*

例 4：他是個聰明人,**很好相處**,就是**學習不認真**。

He is a clever man, a pleasant *companion*, but a careless *student*.

例 5：他年輕的時候**恣愛幻想**，整天**想入非非**。

He was a bit of a *dreamer* when he was young.

例 6：他不是專職**打網球的**，可他網球教得不錯。

He is not a professional *tennis player*, but he is a fine *tennis coach.*

例 7：這小伙子**又能吃又能睡**，整天樂呵呵的。

This young man is a big *eater* and good *sleeper*, cheerful all the time.

二、英語中表達動態的形容詞(verbal adjective)

英語常用動詞的同源形容詞來表達動態意義。

例 1：這人的勇氣**令人欽佩**。

His courage is *admirable*.

例 2：這里氣候**宜人**。

The climate here is *agreeable*.

例 3：讀好書**其樂無窮**。

Nothing is more *enjoyable* than a good book.

例 4：這個問題還得**爭下去**。

This issue remains *arguable.*

例 5：輕微的地震是**感覺不出來**的。

A slight earthquake is hardly *noticeable.*

例 6：這趟旅行**令人愉快**。

The trip was *pleasant.*

例 7：他說他**半個子兒都沒了**。

He said he was *broke.*

例 8：窗子我沒開，我進來的時候就是**開著的**，然後我就讓**它開著了**。

I didn't open the window; it *was open* when I came in and I left it *open*.

例 9：這樣的收音機市場上已經**沒有賣的**了。

This kind of radio is no longer *available* on the market.（*commercially available*）

例 10：造成這些損失的**責任在我**。

I'm *responsible* for these losses.

例 11：我**懷疑**他是否還想出國。

I'm *doubtful* whether he still wants to go abroad.

例 12：全體職工**合作得很好**，總經理向他們表示感謝。

The general manager thanked all the employees because they were very *cooperative*.

例 13：醫生打心里**同情**病人。

The doctor felt *sympathetic* with his patients from the bottom of his heart.

例 14：他當時並**不知道**有警察在場。

He was not *aware* of the presence of a policeman.

例 15：他**博覽群書，知識豐富，講課很風趣**，可是已經**退休了**。

He is *well-read*, *knowledgeable and humorous* when lecturing, but is *retired* now.

三、英語中表示靜態的介詞和介詞短語(prepositional phrase)

例 1：局勢我們已經**控制住了**。

The situation is *under control* now.

例 2：我們這兒**沒頭兒**，所以事故很多。

There have been many accidents because no one is *in charge* here.

例 3：這個節目今天晚上 8：00 到 9：00 **播出**。

The program will be **on** from 8：00 to 9：00 tonight.

例 4：這兒到底是誰**指揮**？是你還是我？

Who is **in command** here? You or I?

例 5：等考試卷子**交齊了**，我就告訴你們答案。

I will tell（show）you the answers when all the papers are **in**.

例 6：這種產品**脫銷**多久了？是去年年底開始的嗎？

How long has this product been **in short supply**? Since the end of last year?

例 7：他同我的一位朋友結婚了，是三年前結的婚。

He **is married** to a friend of mine. They got married three years ago.

例 8：收音機**開著**有多久了？誰開的？

How long has the radio been **on**? Who turned it on?

例 9：消防隊員花了三天三夜才**把火勢控制住**。

It took the firefighters three days and nights to **bring the fire under control.**

例 10：暖氣**來了**已經三個鐘頭了，可是屋子里還是冷颼颼的。

The central heating has been **on** for three hours, but it is still chilly in the room.

例 11：有五家工廠關閉。如果經濟情況不好轉，這些工廠還得**關下去**。

Five factories have closed down. If the economy doesn't pick up, they will **remain closed** .

例 12：我三點鐘就醒了，**一直醒到**天亮。

I woke up at three a. m. and **remained awake** until daybreak.

例 13：這些人**負責**這項工作，他們都**受過良好的教育**。

They are **in charge of** this project（program, work）; they are all **well-educated.**

例 14：你結婚的年齡同你所說的結婚年份不符。說實話，你到底結婚多久了？

The age when you got married doesn't agree with the year you said you got married. Tell me the truth,—how long *have* you *been married*?

　　翻譯動態與靜態時出現的難點仍然要歸因於英漢語言的形合與意合的結構的不同。判斷漢語是動態還是靜態，需要充分理解漢語不必明說的"字里行間"的意思。用英語明確表示這兩種狀態，則需要熟練的表達方式或技巧。這兩種能力源自對漢語和英語不同的思維方式、表達習慣的掌握。熟能生巧，這兩種能力的培養自然離不開平時的觀察和練習。

思考題

1. 在表示靜態和動態時，最大的難點在哪里？
2. 用英語表達靜態狀況時，主要用哪些語法手段代替漢語原文里的動詞？

第十一章　被動語態的翻譯

在漢英翻譯中，被動語態的翻譯一直是比較難以解決的問題。這個困難主要源自兩種思維方式的不同和句子結構的差異。被動語態在英語里是一種常見的語法現象，許多學者指出，在科技文章、新聞報道、官方文件等文章中濫用被動語態現象，幾乎到了泛濫成災的地步。講英語的人習慣用被動語態是有多種原因的，例如，施事者未知而難以言明，或根據上下文可以不言自明或不必言明。還有句法的要求、修辭的考慮和文體的需要等(連淑能，1993)。

與此相反，漢語自古以來很少用被動式，即便是需要表達被動意義，一般也要借助於主動式。古代漢語的被動式是用"為"字或"為……所"結構表示的，如："不為酒困"，"不為謠言所擾"。"被"字是在近代文本中才出現的詞。"被"字有"遭受"的意思，因此，被動式所敘述的事，對主語來說，必須是不如意或不希望發生的事。除了"被"字和"為"字，漢語的被動標記豐富但頗為複雜，最常見的有"遭、所、獲、給、由、把、使、加以、予以、蒙、不得"等。如此多的標記，使漢語被動式的英譯更為不易，因為被動式在漢語中基本上仍是隱形結構，不容易識別。下面我們按照由易到難的順序，分別進行分析。

一、與英語相近的"被"字和"為……所"結構

漢語中最明顯的被動式標記就是"被"字和"為……所"結構，尤其是在現代漢語里，無論是要表達如意事還是不如意事，希望還是不希望的事都可以使用這兩個結構。

例1：他剛上三天班就**被**公司老板給開除了。

He *was dismissed* by the boss just on his third day of work in this company.

例 2： 我真怕**被**人家笑話。

I'm afraid to **be laughed at**.

例 3： 她常常**被**花言巧語所迷惑。

She **is often intoxicated** with sweet words.

例 4： 莊稼**被大水**給衝跑了。

The crops **were washed away** by the flood.

例 5： 我**為**這些話**所**深深感動，後來我把這些話都寫在聖誕賀卡上了。

I **was so moved** by these words that I used them later for a Christmas card.

例 6： 運輸車隊**為**風雪**所**阻。

The transport pool **was held up** by the snowstorm.

例 7： 他的獻身精神**為人所**稱道。

He **was praised** for his spirit of selfless devotion.

二、其他常用的被動式標記

"受到、由、所、獲、給、予以、遭受、不得"和"是……的"或"……的是"結構等是經常用來表示被動式的標記，使用頻率比"被"字還高。

例 1： 美國貿易代表團**受到**熱烈歡迎。

The American trade delegation **was given** a hearty welcome.

例 2： 我們在貴國**受到**隆重而盛情的接待。

We **are received** with so much honor and hospitality in your great country.

例 3： 她為她的兄弟所做的事而**受到**責備。

She **was blamed** for everything her brothers did.

例 4：去年這個地區**遭受到**60 年來最嚴重的旱災。

Last year the region *was visited* by the worst drought in 60 years.

例 5：他的妻子給他寫的信，大多數是**由**醫院里的護士念給他聽的。

Most letters from his wife *are read* to him by the nurses in the hospital.

例 6：這個極其危險的行動是**由**一個年輕、美貌的姑娘組織的。

This most dangerous operation *was organized* by a young attractive girl.

例 7：各國將**由**總理代表來參加會議。

Every country will *be represented* by its prime minister to the conference.

例 8：自然光或所謂的"白光"實際上是**由**許多顏色組成的。

Natural light or "white" light is actually made up of many colors.

例 9：這部電影**獲得**好評。 This movie *was critically acclaimed.*

例 10：未經雙方書面同意，本合同的任何條款**不得**變更或修改。

Any of the articles in this contract shall *not be changed or modified* unless by mutual written consent.

例 11：我的眼鏡**給**人拿走了，我看不清手機上的短信。

I cannot see the text messages since my spectacles *have been taken away.*

例 12：這事必須在適當的時候**予以**處理。

It must *be dealt with* at the appropriate time.

例 13：許多名勝古跡**遭受**連年戰爭的破壞。

A lot of historical sites *were devastated* in successive years of war.

例 14：我的包**讓賊**給偷了。

My wallet *has been stolen.*

例 15：這些飛機是我國製造**的**。

These planes ***are made*** in our country.

例 16：電視廣告是用秒來計價**的**。

TV commercials ***are paid for*** by second.

例 17：推薦我**的是**一位退休老教授。

I've been recommended by a retired professor.

例 18：接見他**的是**個年輕幹部。

He ***was received*** by a young government official.

三、表示被動意義的主動式

王力指出："中國被動式用途之狹,是西洋被動式所比不上的⋯⋯西洋的主動句大多數可轉換成被動式,中國則恰恰相反,主動句大多數是不能轉換成被動式的。"(連淑能,1993)

例 1：他當選為董事長了。

He ***was elected*** chairman of the board.

例 2：這個大學畢業生剛剛 25 歲就提升為公司副經理了。

This college graduate ***was promoted*** to assistant manager of the company when he was only 25 years old.

例 3：大火幾乎使這座有名的賓館毀於一旦。

The famous hotel ***had been practically destroyed*** by the big fire.

例 4：萬一發生索賠,必須在貨到目的地後 30 天內提出,過期不予受理。

Claims, if any, ***must be made*** within 30 days after the arrival of the goods at the destination, after which no claims will ***be entertained.***

人的思維方式決定語言習慣,"根據漢人的思維習慣,人的行為,必然是由人來完成的,事或物不可能完成人的行為。這種不言而喻的思維模式使人們在表達時常常把施事者隱含起來,而把注意力集中在受事者及行為本身,因此,受事者便充當了主語"(連淑能,1993)。

例 5：這本書已譯成多種語言。

This book *has been translated* into many languages.

例 6：大部分問題已經圓滿解決了,只剩下幾個次要問題需要討論。

Most of the problems *have been settled* satisfactorily, only a few problems of second importance remain *to be discussed.*

例 7：當然這項計劃最終還是放棄了。

Eventually, of course the plan *was abandoned.*

例 8：困難克服了,工作完成了,問題也解決了。

The difficulties *have been overcome*, the work *has been finished* and the problem *solved.*

例 9：我的青少年時代是在姥姥家度過的。

My teenage years *were spent* in my grandparents' home.

例 10：彩虹是在陽光透過天空中的小水滴時形成的。

Rainbows *are formed* when sunlight passes through small drops of water in the sky.

四、表示被動意義的無主句

當不需要或不可能說出施事者的時候,漢語往往通過無主句或省略主語來表達被動意義。英語句中不能沒有主語,因此只好採用被動式。

例 1：沒過多久就達成了協議。

After a while an agreement *was arrived at.*

例 2： 當時匆匆忙忙擬定了一個應急計劃。

A contingency plan *was hastily drawn up.*

例 3： 已經為那件事撥了一大筆錢。

A large sum of money *has been put aside* for that purpose.

例 4： 要編好教程,就必須考慮學生不同的興趣愛好。

Various interests of the students *must be given careful consideration* when the course is *to be designed.*

例 5： 為什麼總是把這些麻煩事都推給我呢?

Why should all the unpleasant jobs *be pushed* on to me?

例 6： 出門時必須注意看看窗戶是否關了,門是否鎖好了。

Care *should be taken* to see that the windows *are closed* and the door *is properly locked* when you leave home.

五、通稱或泛稱的運用

當難以講明施事者時,漢語常常採用通稱(generic person)或泛稱(general term)做主語,如"有人"、"人們"、"大家"、"人家"、"別人"、"某人"等。英語也有相應的不定代詞(如 one, some, any, every, all, somebody, anybody, everybody 等),但其用途與漢語的通稱不盡相同。英語在許多情況下寧可採用被動式也不用這類代詞做主語,如大量的非人稱被動式(impersonal passive)用 it 做主語(連淑能,1993)。例如:

1. 運用通稱或泛稱

有人主張……	It is asserted that…
有人覺得……	It is believed that…
大家認為……	It is generally considered that…
眾所周知……	It is well known that…
有人會說……	It will be said that…

有人曾說……　　　　　　　It was told that...

例 1：**有人**看見工人們在修理機器。

The workers *were seen* repairing the machine.

例 2：**人人**都把他看做英雄，可他認為自己僅僅是個普通市民。

He *was regarded* as a hero, even though he has always thought of himself as an ordinary citizen.

例 3：**人們**必須聯繫世界環境去應對全球變暖問題。

The problem of global warming has *to be dealt with* in a world environmental context.

2. 無主語被動式

希望……	It is hoped that...
據報……	It is reported that...
據說……	It is said that...
據推測……	It is supposed that...
必須承認……	It must be admitted that...
必須指出……	It must be pointed out that...
由此可見……	It will be seen from this that...
可以毫不誇張地說……	It may be said without fear of exaggeration that...

例 1：**希望**我們能夠團結合作，順利完成任務。

It is hoped that we will get united and work cooperatively to accomplish our project.

例 2：**據說**他們 20 年前就在美國定居了。

It is said that they settled down in America 20 years ago.

例 3：**必須指出的是**，要想學好翻譯，應該先學會用中英文寫作。

It must be pointed out that we should first learn to write in both Chinese and English before learning translation.

六、漢語和英語中自身帶有被動意義的詞

在英語中有少量動詞本身就有被動意義,如 feel, taste, sell, dress, read 等。

例 1：這種手機十分**暢銷**。

This type of mobile phone *sells* like hot cakes.

例 2：他總是**穿得**很得體。

He always *dresses* decently.

例 3：現在的襪子很不**禁穿**。

Socks nowadays don't *wear* well.

例 4：他的文章**讀起來**像翻譯。

His articles *read* like translation.

例 5：這種料子手感很柔軟。(無謂語動詞)

This material *feels* very soft.

例 6：鷄湯味道很鮮。(無謂語動詞)

The chicken soup *tastes* delicious.

總之,雖然漢語表達被動語態的方式是多種多樣的,但在翻譯成英文時,往往不容易識別。這就需要譯者充分掌握兩種語言的不同表達方式,才能得心應手。

思考題

1. 在表示被動語態時,漢語多用主動式,英語多用被動式,原因何在?
2. 把漢語中的被動意義譯成英語,難點在哪里?

第十二章　名詞的翻譯

　　名詞往往被誤認為是比較容易翻譯的詞類。實踐表明,如果不了解漢英兩種語言在名詞運用中也存在很大的差異,漢語名詞的英譯仍會給譯者造成一定的困難。這個困難源自兩種語言的形合與意合結構上的差別:漢語的名詞沒有表示單復數、特指與泛指的明確標記,而英語的名詞卻離不開這些標記。例如:

　　明天我們**開會**,**會上一位老翻譯來講座**,談**翻譯理論的最新發展,題目**是"直譯還是意譯"。

　　We are going to have *a* meeting tomorrow. In *the* meeting *an* old translator will give *a* lecture on *the* latest development of translation theor*ies*. *The* topic of his lecture is "Literal Translation or Free Translation".

　　因此,在翻譯一個名詞之前我們必須問自己兩個問題:①這個名詞是單數還是復數 (singular or plural)? ②這個名詞是特指還是泛指 (specific or general)?

一、單數與復數

　　無論是在筆頭還是口語交際中,除非必須講明數字,漢語名詞是用不著標明單復數的。我們憑借上下文或經驗就可以做出判斷,但在英譯中卻必須在形式上表明。例如:

例1:我特愛看**電影**。
　　I love *movies.*

例 2：**蘋果**多少錢一公斤？

How much is a kilo of *apples*?

例 3：我現在正忙著找**工作**呢。

I'm busy looking for *a job.*

　　在漢英翻譯中，容易出問題的名詞有抽象名詞、由動詞轉換的名詞、集合名詞和物質名詞。下面我們分別分析一下它們的難點所在。

1. 抽象名詞的翻譯（abstract nouns）

　　一般來講,英語中的抽象名詞沒有復數形式,例如:

例 1：以**史**為鑒。

Learn from *history*.

例 2：**歷史**給了我們許多教訓。

History teaches us a lot of lessons.

例 3：中國人愛**和平**。

The Chinese love *peace*.

例 4：這個人**觀察力**敏銳。

He is a man of keen *insight.*

例 5：貧窮不是**社會主義**。

Socialism doesn't mean shortages.

例 6：電話出毛病了？干嗎不叫**維修的**來？

Something has gone wrong with the telephone? Why don't you call *maintenance*?

例 7：會議討論的問題同大家都有關係,例如,**工資、退休、醫療**。

What was discussed in the meeting concerned all of us: *pay* , *retirement* , and *medical care.*

例 8：這家商店**生意**興隆。

This store is doing good ***business.***

例 9：**人才外流**嚴重，得想辦法遏制。

We must find ways to stop this serious ***brain-drain.***

例 10：強有力的領導，健全的法制是**發展經濟**不可或缺的。

Economic growth depends on a strong leadership and effective legal system.

　　但在翻譯比較複雜的抽象名詞時，我們有可能很難決定是用單數還是復數。漢語中有些抽象名詞雖然意思相近，但在英語中必須加上復數形式予以區別。比較下列幾組句子中的名詞：

例 11：我認為她沒有干這個工作的**經驗**。

I don't think she has the ***experience*** for the job.

(experience ＝ enough knowledge and skill suitable for the job)

聽聽她當警察的**經歷**非常有意思。

It is very interesting hearing about her ***experiences*** as a policewoman.

(experiences ＝ things that happened to her)

例 12：最近揭露出來的腐敗現象動搖了很多人對警察的**信賴**。

Recent revelations about corruption have shaken many people's ***belief*** in the police.

所有主張非暴力的宗教**信仰**和政治**信仰**都應受到尊敬。

All non-violent religious and political ***beliefs*** should be respected equally.

例 13：編寫這些書的目的是促進兒童讀寫技能的**發展**。

These books are designed to help children with the ***development*** of their skills of reading and writing.

如果事情有了什麼新的**發展**，打電話告訴我。

Call me and let me know if there have been any new ***developments.***

(A development is a recent important event which is the latest in a series of related events.)

例 14：保持課堂**紀律**是每個教師的首要任務。

Maintaining classroom ***discipline*** is the first task of every teacher.

我不太喜歡理論性太強的**學科**。

I don't enjoy over-theoretical *disciplines*.

例 15：承認犯了錯是**堅強**的表示，不是軟弱的象徵。

Admitting you've made a mistake is a sign of *strength*, not weakness.

他的**強項**是有決心和樂觀的性格。

His greatest *strengths* are determination and revelation.

例 16："**溝通**"指交換看法；"**交通**"指陸海空運輸。

"*Communication*" means interchange of ideas；"*communications*" refers to transportation by land，sea and air.

例 17：他詩作的**優美之處**，吸引了很多年輕讀者。

The *beauty* of his poems has attracted many young readers.

她們在年輕的時候可都是**美人**。

They were real *beauties* when they were young.（具體名詞）

2. 由動詞轉換的名詞的翻譯（verb-turned-nouns）

在英語中有一類由動詞轉換來的名詞，雖然是名詞，但仍帶有一些動詞的性質，而且總是以單數形式出現，例如：

inform→information　　　　　guide→guidance

equip→equipment　　　　　understand→understanding

know→knowledge　　　　　transport→transportation

例 1：做生意成功與否主要靠**信息**。

Success in business depends on *information*.

例 2：工廠的**設備**全部是進口的。

All the *equipment* in the factory is imported from abroad.

例 3：這個目擊者**堅持說不知道**撞車的事。

The witness denies any *knowledge* of the car crash.

例 **4**：我寫碩士論文時，我的導師給了我很多有益的**指導**。

My professor gave me a lot of helpful *guidance* while I was writing up my MA thesis.

例 **5**：對於政治，她是**一竅不通**。

She doesn't have any *understanding* of politics.

例 **6**：在這個城市，有很多公司鼓勵職工出門不開車，而用其他**交通**工具。

In this city many companies encourage their employees to use alternative means of *transportation* , rather than the car.

3. 集合名詞的翻譯 (collective nouns)

英語中有些名詞本身就是復數，如：crew，people，family，staff，police，audience 等。

例 **1**：九名**機組人員**全部遇難。

The *crew* of nine were killed in the air crash.

例 **2**：今天上午有**兩個人**找你。

Two *people* looked for you this morning.

例 **3**：我**全家人**都喜歡看書。

All my *family* enjoy reading.

例 **4**：我是這個學校的**職工**。

I'm on the *staff* of this school.

例 **5**：這個地區**警力**不足。

The *police* are under-staffed in this district.

例 **6**：戲演到一半就有 30 多個**觀眾**退場了。

More than thirty in the *audience* left when the performance was only half way through.

例 7：英語系有將近 70 名**教職工**。

The English Department has a ***faculty and staff*** of about 70 members.

4. 物質名詞的翻譯（mass nouns）

物質名詞是英語特有的一類名詞,如：chalk, paper, chocolate 等,這類名詞不可數,沒有復數形式。漢語中這類名詞沒有特殊歸類。

例 1：在我們學校,教師上課已經不用**粉筆**了。

In our school teachers do not use ***chalk*** any more in their teaching.

例 2：我們國家曾經嚴重缺**紙**。

There used to be an acute shortage of ***paper*** in our country.

例 3：這種蛋糕的主要成分是**巧克力**。

The ingredient of this kind of cake is largely ***chocolate***.

例 4：**光**比**聲音**快。***Light*** travels faster than ***sound***.

例 5：**銀**屬於貴金屬。***Silver*** is a precious metal.

例 6：魚離開**水**是活不了的。

Water is a necessity to fish.

例 7：如今連咱們那個小山村都通**電**了。

Electricity is available even in our small mountainous village.

例 8：買**黃油**的時候,要看看生產日期,買**香油**就不必了。

You should look at the production date before you buy ***butter***, but that won't be necessary if it's ***sesame oil***.

例 9：這部電影是用國產**膠片**拍的。

This movie was made on Chinese-made ***film***.

二、特指與泛指

　　初學英語的人一開始學名詞,就涉及這個問題。定冠詞 the 表示特指,不定冠詞 a 表示泛指,這個概念所有的英語教程都會提到。但是,在用英文寫作文和進行漢英翻譯時,即便是多年學習英語的人,恰當地用好冠詞也是很不容易的事。其根源是漢語表示這兩個概念的方式與英語不同,漢語中不存在明確表示特指或泛指概念的特定標記。在很多場合,漢語是靠詞的順序來表示這兩個概念的,例如:

例 1：老李,來**客人**啦!

　　Mr. Li, you have *a* visitor!（講話人事先不知道老李有客人要來。）

　　老李,**客人**來啦!

　　Mr. Li, *the* visitor has come!（講話人事先知道老李有客人要來。）

例 2：今天我吃**蘋果**了。

　　I've had *an* apple today.（可能有人建議講話人每天吃個蘋果。）

　　蘋果我吃了。

　　I've had *the* apple.（可能有人問某個蘋果誰吃了。）

　　但在多數情況下,表示這兩個概念的標記不明顯,我們只能**靠上下文和語感來判斷**了。請看下面這兩段對話:

對話一:

A:我的車丟了。　　　　　　　　　　My Car has been stolen.

B:哪輛車呀? 你們家不是有兩輛嗎?　Which one? You have two, right?

A:就是我每天開著上班的那輛。　　　It's *the* one I drove to work every day.

B:真可惜,那可是輛好車。　　　　　What a shame! It's *a* nice car.

對話二:

A:在這兒看什麼呢?　　　　　　　　What are you looking at?

B:看汽車。　　　　　　　　　　　　*Cars.*

A:瞧見紅旗了嗎?　　　　　　　　　Have you seen *any* Red Flag?

B:瞧見了,剛才過去的那輛就是。　　Yes, *the* one that has passed by.

比較下列例句中的名詞：

例 3：**手電筒**在哪兒？沒有**手電筒**我什麼也看不見。

Where is *the flashlight*? I can't see anything without *a flashlight*.

例 4：別把**香蕉**放在冰箱里，**香蕉**是不能放在冰箱里的。

Don't put *these bananas* in the fridge. *Bananas* can't be stored there.

例 5：這間教室用做多媒體**語音室**，別看小，**里邊**裝配有先進設備。

This classroom is used as *a* multi-media *laboratory*. Though small, *the laboratory* is equipped with advanced facilities.

例 6：過生日別送他**小提琴**，他根本不拉**小提琴**。

Don't give him *a violin* on his birthday. He doesn't play *the violin*.

例 7：是您上周從我們書店訂購了**本書**嗎？**書**已經到了。

You ordered *a book* from our bookstore, didn't you? *The book* has arrived.

例 8：孩子們正看的**飛機**是架噴氣式的。

The plane the children are watching is *a jet*.

例 9：好多麥子都讓**那場雨**給毀了。現在我們最不缺的就是**雨**了。

A lot of wheat was damaged by *the rain*. We don't need *rain* anymore.

1. 表示泛指事物的名詞

一般來講，**泛指的事物是對話中第一次提到的事物，或沒有具體所指的事物。**

例 1：北京冬天**樹**是光禿禿的。

In winter, *trees* in Beijing are bare.

例 2：她是三個孩子的**母親**。

She is *a mother* of three children.

例 3：現在多數中國人還買不起**汽車**，不過也有一家買兩輛的。

Most Chinese cannot afford *a car* yet. But some families have two cars.

例 4：要買**車**，你想買什麼樣的?

If you plan to buy *a car*, what type do you like?

例 5：北京過春節已經不再禁放**鞭炮**了。

Firecrackers are no longer banned in Beijing on Spring Festival.

例 6：**孩子**嘛，總歸是**孩子**。

Children will always be *children.*

例 7：那年雲南**地震**了，因為是在白天，所以沒有傷亡。

An earthquake that hit Yunnan Province caused no casualties because it happened in daytime.

例 8：**洗衣機**、**電視機**、甚至**小轎車**對中國城市居民來說已不算奢侈品了。

Washing machines, *TV sets* and even *cars* are not luxuries for residents in Chinese cities.

例 9：解決北京交通擁堵最好的辦法是修**地鐵**。

The best way to solve the problems of traffic jams in Beijing is to build *underground railways.*

例 10：我們是代表學校參賽的**選手**。

We are *players* representing our school.

例 11：**戰爭**有正義和非正義的區別，我贊成前者，反對後者。

There are *just wars* and *unjust wars*; I'm for the former and opposed to the latter.

例 12：你知道哪個**地方河流**沒有被污染?

Do you know of any *place* where *rivers* are not polluted?

例 13：請出示身分證,我是**警察**。

Show me your ID card, I'm *a policeman.*

例 14：書我是不借給人的,不過對你是**例外**。

I never lend my books to others, but you are *an exception.*

例 15：這些學生由於**課堂表現**突出受到獎勵。

These students were awarded for *outstanding performances* in class.

例 16：帶著孩子不要到**人多的地方**去。

Avoid *crowds* when you have your kids with you.

2. 表示特指事物的名詞

特指的事物一般是對話雙方都知道或應該知道的事,在英語中要用定冠詞 **the** 表示。

例 1：**這家工廠的產品**是一流的,就是價格太高。
The products of the factory are first-rate in quality, but too expensive.

例 2：**半決賽**明天開始。
The semi-finals will begin tomorrow.

例 3：這是去太原的**長途汽車**嗎?
Is this *the coach* to Taiyuan?

例 4：把你剛買的**手機**給我看看。
Show me *the cell phone* you have just bought.

例 5：英語系**辦公室**就在**四樓**。
The general office of the English Department is on *the fourth floor.*

例 6：把**晾著的衣服**收進來吧,要下雨了。
Take in *the washing.* It's going to rain.

例 7： 調查得怎麼樣了？會不會起訴嫌疑人？

How is *the investigation* going? Will *the suspects* be prosecuted?

例 8： 實驗進行得還順利，只是頭幾天出了點問題。

The experiment has been going on quite smoothly, except for some problems in the first few days.

例 9： 掌聲差點兒把房頂給掀翻了。

The applause almost brought down *the house.*

例 10： 這本書里的內容是他在戰爭中的經歷。

The book is about his war experiences.

例 11： 在採訪的時候，他對這問題未置可否。

During *the interview*, he made no comment on this issue.

例 12： 把這些錢放在一塊兒就是一大筆。

It will be a large sum when all *the money* is put together.

例 13： 河只有 30 米寬，但水流湍急，兩岸又都是懸崖峭壁，只有飛鳥才能過去。

The river is only 30 meters wide, but *the current* is so swift and *the cliffs* on *its banks* are so steep (that) only birds can fly across it.

還有一種特指事物是**在某種特定環境中是唯一的人或物**。例如：

例 14： 現在誰是美國國務卿？她當過外交官嗎？

Who is *the US Secretary of State* now? Was she in the foreign service?

例 15： 一句話里邊，主謂語要一致，也就是說，在單復數和人稱方面要一致。

The predicate should agree with *the subject* of a sentence in number and person.

例 16： 許多證據都說明他有罪，可是陪審團卻說他無罪。

There was a lot of evidence showing he was guilty, but *the jury* brought in a "not guilty" verdict.

　　當然,漢語中也不是絕對沒有表示特指和泛指事物的詞,如表示特指的有"這個"、"那個"、"這些"、"那些"等,表示泛指的有"某個"、"某些"、"一個"、"一些"等。但是,在日常交往中,中國人是不習慣老把它們放在嘴邊的。經常使用這些表達方式讓人覺得啰唆、多餘、帶有洋腔。所以在漢譯英中遇到這些問題,我們必須有意識地強化名詞單復數、特指與泛指的概念,否則,英譯文讀者就會覺得你的譯文意思模糊,甚至不知所雲了。

思考題

1. 中國人不經常使用表示名詞單復數、特指和泛指事物的詞,為什麼不影響人際溝通?

2. 漢語中沒有表示名詞單復數、特指和泛指事物的詞是否意味著中國人思維不精確?

第十三章　選詞的技巧

　　初學翻譯的人往往自翻譯始便急於查字典,尋找漢語原文中某詞在英語里相對應的詞,然後寫在漢字旁邊,接著一路查來,待到落實到筆頭時,才突然發現詞不能達意。這種做法多半是由於我們在學英語時死記單詞的錯誤方式造成的。很多學生都是簡單地按照課文後面的單詞表背單詞,把某個英文詞在本篇課文中所表達的具體的漢語意義,作為這個英文詞的全部意義而緊緊地鎖在一起。似乎每個英文詞都與某個漢語詞完全對等,從而忽視了某個詞的其他含義。結果使這個英文詞負載了這個漢語詞的全部意義和文化內涵,在以後的閱讀中遇到這個英文詞時便沿著慣性思維的軌跡滑向記憶中的對等漢語詞匯,忽視了該英文詞在新語境中的新意義,造成理解錯誤。其實,詞義只有在語境中才能確定。因此,詞匯選擇應該在整個篇章的主題和句子的框架確定之後進行。

　　詞匯的選擇與推敲最能體現翻譯水平的高低,也最能體現譯者對整個翻譯過程和不同語境的掌握程度。詞匯意義往往體現在內涵外延、語體色彩、褒貶含義等方面。在多數情況下,原漢語詞匯在漢語語境中的語義不能原封不動地再現於英語語境。如僅根據字面意思對譯,很可能導致譯文不準確,甚至誤譯。我們應特別注意漢英詞匯間表面相似、其實不同的假對應關係。譯者應有意識地注意漢英詞匯之間的對應與非對應的關係,根據語境來確定準確的英語表達方式。語境大致可分為四種:文本語境(verbal context),交際場合語境(physical context),文化語境(cultural context)和歷史語境(historical context)。

一、文本語境(verbal context)

　　最常見的語境是文本語境,即譯者所譯材料中的上下文。文本語境對於選詞有著極為重要的意義。

下面的幾組實例可以清楚地說明這一點：

1. 罵

例 1：他說話就**罵街**。

He always *swears.*

例 2：魯迅愛**罵人**。

Lu Xun often *criticized* people.

例 3：他動不動就**罵人**。

He tends to *call people names.*

漢語中的"罵"字在不同的語境中，出自不同的人，會有不同的意思，不能一概翻譯成 scold。例 1 中的"罵街"其實是"說話帶臟字"的意思；例 2 中的"罵人"意指"批評"；例 3 中的"罵人"的意思是"侮辱人"。

2. 吃

中國飲食文化的發達極大地影響著日常漢語，我們經常把"吃"字放在嘴邊，如："吃透原文"，"秀色可餐"等，但是英文中卻沒有這個習慣，這就需要我們注意這一文化差別。

例 1：現在誰還願意**吃大鍋飯**？

Nowadays who still wants to get equal pay for unequal work, *like eating from the same big rice-pot*?

例 2：我們不能**吃老本**，要立新功。

We shouldn't *live off our past gains*, but make new achievements.

例 3：他這種人在學校里**吃不開**。

This sort of person *doesn't have a place* in school.

例 4：這小子是**吃軟不吃硬**。

This guy is *susceptible to persuasion rather than coercion.*

例 5：我也不願意在家**吃閒飯**，可就是找不到工作。

I don't want to *stay idle* at home, but how can I get a job?

例 6：考試千萬不能作弊，否則**吃不了兜著走**。

Don't you ever cheat in an exam, or you'll *land yourself in serious trouble.*

例 7：上星期考試，有三個人吃了鴨蛋。

Three students *got zero* in the exam last week.

例 8：你別看他不愛說話，在公司里還挺**吃香**。

Although he is such a quiet person, he is *well liked* in the company.

3. 人山人海

例 1：廟會上**人山人海**的，他把孩子給丟了。

He lost his child in *a sea of people* at the temple fair.

例 2：車站上**人山人海**，人們不得不把牌子舉得高高的。

Placards are raised above *a sea of heads* outside the railway station.

例 3：海灘上真是**人山人海**啊！

The beach is *swarming with* people.

例 4：大街上**人山人海**，擠滿了遊行的人。

There are *great multitudes of demonstrators* along the avenue.

例 5：體育場門口擠得**人山人海**，我根本進不去。

The crowd is so *densely packed* at the gate of the stadium that I can scarcely push my way through.

【分析】雖然"人山人海"總是用來形容"人非常多"，但是語境不同，人多的場景、狀態和重心也不盡相同。例 1 中的重點就是"人很多";例 2 中人們在車站上首先看到的是"人頭攢動",重心在於"把牌子舉過頭頂";例 3 中的人群是動態的,是"在海灘上涌動"的意思,帶有一定的貶義,意指"人過多";例 4 要突出"遊行的人多";例 5 要突出"擁擠的狀態"。

4. 九霄雲外

例 1：我在同他說話的時候,他的腦子好像早已跑到**九霄雲外**去了。

His mind *seemed to be far away* when I talked to him.

例 2：他早把我的話拋到了**九霄雲外**。

He has *clean forgotten* my advice.

例 3：他喝多了就把警察的警告拋到了**九霄雲外**。

Whenever he is drunk, he will *throw the police's caution to the winds.*

【分析】"九霄雲外"用來形容"非常遙遠"或"無影無蹤"。例 1 中的"九霄雲外"表示談話對象"心不在焉";例 2 和例 3 都取"無影無蹤"之意,指"把……忘得一干二淨"。

以下譯例都是我們常見的、容易望文生義而譯錯的詞或短語,這里不做詳細解釋。

5. 凍

例 1：湖面**凍**冰了。

The lake *is frozen* on the surface.

例 2：馬路上**凍**冰了。

There is ice on the road.

例 3：我的手都**凍**了。

My hands are *frostbitten.*

例4：小心別**凍**著。

Take care or you'll *catch cold.*

例5：這些土豆都**凍**壞了。

These potatoes were *damaged by frost.*

例6：別忘了把肉**凍**上。

Don't forget to *put* the meat *in the freezer.*

6. 發展

例1：我們又**發展**了十個新會員。

We have *recruited* ten new members.

例2：希望海峽兩岸更快地**發展**各項民間往來。

It is hoped that people-to-people exchanges will be *promoted* faster in various fields between the two sides of the Taiwan Strait.

例3：這個小伙子有**發展**前途。

This young man *has good prospects.*

例4：我們要用**發展**的眼光看待後進學生。

We must look at those students lagging behind by *taking into account their possible changes in the future.*

例5：成立英語學院說明我們的教學和科研**發展**到了一個新階段。

The establishment of the School of English Language, Literature and Culture indicates that our teaching and research has *reached* a new stage.

例6：**發展**體育運動,增強人民體質。

Promote physical culture and build up people's health.

7. 意見

例 1：請提寶貴**意見**。

Leave your valuable *comments.*

例 2：你提的**意見**很好。

It's a good *suggestion.*

例 3：我對他辦事很**有意見**。

I *don't like* the way he goes about things.

例 4：我對他**沒什麼意見**。

I have *nothing against* him.

例 5：顧客對這個商店的服務很**有意見**。

Customers *complain loudly* about the bad service of the shop.

8. 休息

例 1：**幕間休息**20 分鐘。

There is *an interval* of 20 minutes.

例 2：**課間休息**的時候再來電話。

Please call back during *the break.*

例 3：郵局星期天**不休息**。

The post office is *open* on Sundays.

例 4：今天我**休息**。

It's my *day-off* today.

9. 主觀

例 1：他的判斷非常**主觀**。

His judgment is very ***subjective.***

例 2：這只不過是我的**主觀願望**。

This is just my ***wishful thinking.***

例 3：他的計劃完全是**主觀想象**。

His plan is ***unrealistic.***

例 4：你這人辦事**太主觀**。

You always go about things ***your own way.***

例 5：遇到挫折，要多找找**主觀原因**。

When you suffer a setback, you should try to find the causes for which ***you yourself are responsible.***

例 6：這次考試有一半題是**主觀題**。

In this exam, half of the ***questions have more than one answer.***

10. 意思

例 1：這本書真**有意思**。

This book is very ***interesting.***

例 2：這個詞有幾個**意思**？

How many ***meanings*** does this word have?

例 3：這是對你好心相助所表示的一點**小意思**。

This is a slight ***acknowledgement*** for your kind help.

例 4：她瞅了一下手錶，**意思**是我該走了。

She glanced at her watch to **give me a hint** that I should leave.

例 5：他們要結婚了，咱們買個禮物**意思意思**。

They are going to get married. Let's buy a wedding present to express our **congratulations**.

二、交際場合語境（physical context）

交際場合語境是說話或寫作的時間、地點以及講話人或作者身邊正在進行的活動。這種語境在翻譯公示語方面起著很大的作用。例如：

例 1：正在播音　On Air

例 2：起重臂下，嚴禁站人　Keep Clear Away

例 3：前方施工，請繞行　Road Work Ahead

例 4：衣著不整，請勿入內　The right of admission is reserved

例 5：高高興興上班去，平平安安回家來　Watch out for the traffic

例 6：請勿疲勞駕駛　Tiredness can kill

三、歷史語境（historical context）

歷史語境指的是所譯的詞語只是在過去某個時期才有意義，不能按照常識翻譯。例如：

例 1：上山下鄉知識青年

re-educated youths through farm work during the "Cultural Revolution" (1966 – 1976)

例 2：老三屆

high-school graduates in 1966, 1967 and 1968

例 3：工農兵學員

college students selected from the army, factories and farms

例 4：解放後

since the founding of the People's Republic of China

四、文化語境（cultural context）

文化語境指的是在某個國家、民族或地區所特有的環境。在這個環境裏所發生的事，有較強的民族性和特殊性，反應了某一社會群體的生活方式。一個民族的獨特性在很大程度上取決於這個民族的文化重點（cultural emphasis）。而文化重點"又直接影響一種語言中詞匯的多寡、特化程度和分化程度"（柯平，1993:81）。漢英翻譯中碰到的困難，大半來源於東方和西方文化重點上的差異。例如，中國人歷來重視購物方式，所買的東西不同，說法也就不同：

採購商品，買點兒東西，抓藥，扯布料，割點兒肉，打酒，挑個西瓜，揀兩塊豆腐，添件家具，淘換點兒土産

西方人不太講究這些形式，以上這些表達法都可以譯作 buy 或 purchase。另外，中國人講究幼時的友誼、老年人的閱歷、兒女的孝順、丈夫的才干和妻子的賢惠，認為有了這些便有了"造化"，因而出現了不少這樣的詞匯。漢語用單個詞表達的概念，英語可能要兜圈子來表達。例如：

例 1：真正的朋友，恐怕要算"**總角之交**"或"**竹馬之交**"了。

Real friendship between two persons originates perhaps from the time of life *when they were children playing together*.

例 2：我這麼說可不是**倚老賣老**。

Don't take me as *showing off my seniority.*

例 3：老太太真**有造化**，兒子媳婦都這麼**孝順**。

The old lady has *the good fortune* to be *cared for by her loving* sons and their wives.

例 4：老張真**有福氣**，娶了這麼**賢惠的**老婆。

Mr. Zhang has the ***good fortune*** to marry such a ***good*** woman.

例 5：我一直想找個**能干的好男人**，可就是沒這個**福分**。

I've been longing to marry ***a good man***, but so far haven't got such ***a happy lot***.

例 6：按中國的傳統，不**贍養**父母讓人**瞧不起**。

By the Chinese traditional value, those who do not ***support*** their parents ***are despised***.

另外，中國人講話或者寫文章常常引用一些典故，在英譯時既要讓譯文讀者看懂所表達的意思，又要讓他們了解中國人獨特的表達方式。這就必須採取直譯加說明的方式翻譯。例如：

例 7：一葉知秋。

The first fallen leaves announce the arrival of autumn.

A small sign can point to the great trend.

例 8：橘逾淮而變枳。

Oranges would lose their sweet taste if planted to north China.

The environment determines the quality of people.

例 9：春江水暖鴨先知。

Swimming ducks are the first to know the arrival of spring.

Knowledge begins with proximity.

五、慣用語匯（stock expressions）的選擇

在確定漢語詞義時，要考慮漢語語境；在漢英轉換時，就要注重英語語境。具體地講，就是要以英語國家和民族的語言習慣為出發點，選擇他們平日常用的現有詞匯。例如：

	漢語慣用法	英語慣用法
1	歪打正著	dumb luck
2	售完為止	while supply lasts
3	人造雨	to seed the clouds
4	追尾	a head-tail collision
5	迎頭相撞	a head-on collision
6	故意輸球	to tank a game
7	室內劇	sit-com
8	高射炮	anti-aircraft guns
9	(長途汽車)售票處	ticket-office
10	(電影院)售票處	box-office
11	(兒童)三輪車	tricycle
12	(載人)三輪車	pedicab
13	現在播送新聞。	Now the news.
14	新聞播送完了。	That's the news.
15	環保型社會	environment-friendly society
16	便於使用的電腦	user-friendly computer

再看以下例句：

例 1： 明代造的那些房子，現在已經**不復存在**了。

The houses that were built in the Ming Dynasty *are gone* now.

例 2： 他在這個小山村里住了 50 年，對村里的**一草一木**都很熟悉。

Having been a resident in this small mountainous village for 50 years, he knows it *like the back of his hand.*

例 3： 他為人慷慨，**群眾關係**很好。

He is *well-liked* for his generosity.

例 4： 中國人民**擰成一股繩**，勤奮工作，為的是建設和諧社會。

The Chinese people, *united as one*, are striving to build a harmonious society.

例 5：千百萬山區人民終於**擺脫了貧困**。

Millions of the people in the mountainous areas have finally *got rid of poverty.*

例 6：什麼叫**君子**？什麼叫**小人**？

What is a *gentleman* and what is a *mean person*?

例 7：這事如果他不同意，我們不能**做主**。

We cannot *make any decision*, if he thinks differently.

例 8：你真是叫人**望眼欲穿**。

You are *a sight for sore eyes.*

例 9：這個人**撒謊成性**。

He's a *habitual liar.* (It is his *second nature* to lie. He's *born a liar.*)

例 10：一個老師連這樣的問題都答不上來，**豈不寒磣**？

Isn't it *embarrassing* for a teacher not able to answer such a simple question?

例 11：他干活總是**留個尾巴**。

He always *leaves* his work *half-done.*

例 12：你沒有**家累**，不然你不可能這麼清閒。

You don't have a family *to support*, or you couldn't afford to be so idle.

　　人類所處的客觀自然環境大體上講是一樣的，但是不同的民族描述、解釋他們所處的環境的方式又不盡相同。因此，只有靠譯者對兩種語言的表達習慣的敏銳洞察力和平日的觀察、積累，才能找到兩種表達方式在語境和意思上的接點，從而產生地道的譯文。

思考題

1. 在翻譯之前，除了要考慮文本語境、交際場合語境、文化語境和歷史語境外，還要考慮哪些因素？
2. 選詞"地道"的定義是什麼？什麼樣的譯文才稱得上"地道"？

第二部分 句子翻譯

第六章　主語的確定

第七章　連動式的處理

第八章　從屬信息的翻譯

第九章　虛擬語氣的翻譯

第十章　静態和動態的翻譯

第十一章　被動語態的翻譯

第十二章　名詞的翻譯

第十三章　選詞的技巧

第十四章　篇章翻譯的基本步驟

　　篇章翻譯的**第一步是閱讀全篇**。以翻譯為目的的閱讀方式既不同於以欣賞為目的的念詩、看小說、讀散文，又不同於以獲取信息為目的的讀報、看雜志，也不同於以學習為目的讀書、看教材。為了翻譯而進行的閱讀需要譯者更加精心、細心、耐心，需要譯者對所譯材料進行全方位的審視。要想翻譯好一篇文章，起碼要對原文閱讀三遍：①**通讀，以了解全篇內容大意**；②**精讀，以確定全篇的寫作目的、中心思想**；③**重點讀，以掌握文本的寫作特點**。

　　篇章翻譯的**第二步是對全文的內容按照信息層次，即意群**（group of meaning）**進行切分**。切分的原因是漢英兩種語言在布局謀篇方面存在著巨大差異：漢語一般愛用短句、流水句，結構松散，敘述按時間順序、因果關係進行，以"線性"方式依次排開；而英語則是論點突出、論據為輔，以"立體"方式進行綜合敘述。

　　如果在未走這兩步之前就忙於查字典，即刻動筆翻譯，結果把過多的精力放在了個別詞句上，這樣就會"一葉障目，不見泰山"。篇章翻譯的**第三步，才是選詞組句**。請看下列譯例：

》 例文一

《武訓傳》劇情介紹

原文：

　　●影片講述了清朝時山東省東柳鎮貧苦孩子武訓的故事。●他五歲喪父，隨母親乞討度日，●七歲好不容易攢了兩百個銅錢想進入私塾讀書，卻被富家子弟趕出校門。●生活的遭遇使他深感窮人不識字便沒有出路。於是，成年後，武訓開始乞討興辦義學。為了讓窮孩子能夠讀書，●他裝瘋賣傻三十年，每天在街上唱歌賣藝，甚至為了討錢，任人驅打。●他不知道自己的義舉能否真正改變社會。他只能告訴孩子們"將來長大了，千萬不要忘記咱們莊稼人！"

譯文：

Story of Wu Xun

The movie tells a story of Wu Xun, a beggar of Dongliu Town, Shandong Province, in the Qing Dynasty(1616-1911), who helps poor children to get an education.

Born in a poor family in Shandong, Wu Xun is five years old when his father dies, leaving him panhandling with his mother. One day, at the age of seven, with 200 coppers he has scraped as a beggar entertainer, he goes to a school, asking for admission, only to be taunted and get thrown out. Believing that poor people will never have a chance in life unless they learn to read and write, he starts a school offering free education to children of poor families. For funds, he depends on the handouts he earns by singing foolishly comic songs and offering himself for physical abuse. He does that for as long as thirty years. He does not know that the poor cannot improve their lot without a change of the society; all he does is to keep telling the children, "Never turn your back to the poor folk when you grow up."

1. 意群切分

整個段落可分為六個意群,分別具有不同的功能:

意群(1)

影片講述了清朝時山東省東柳鎮貧苦孩子武訓的故事。

The movie tells a story of Wu Xun, a beggar of Dongliu Town, Shandong Province, in the Qing Dynasty,who helps poor children to get an education.

【分析】雖然這個意群只有一句話,但卻起著提綱挈領的作用,它告訴讀者整篇文本的中心思想和主要內容,相當於一篇文章的內容提要。漢語原文中沒有用文字表明 who helps poor children to get an education,這是譯者在通讀了全篇之後加進去的,目的是給譯文讀者以思想準備,因為英語的表述習慣是重要的事情先說,所以在譯文中一定要首先點明主題。

意群(2)

他五歲喪父,隨母親乞討度日,

Born in a poor family in Shandong, Wu Xun is five years old when his father dies, leaving him panhandling with his mother.

【分析】這句話主要講的是武訓五歲時的生活狀況,上句的"貧苦孩子"挪到了這句中。此句的主語是武訓,"喪父"是次要信息,作為狀語譯出。

意群(3)

七歲好不容易攢了兩百個銅錢想進入私塾讀書,卻被富家子弟趕出校門。

One day, at the age of seven, with 200 coppers he has scraped as a beggar entertainer, he goes to a school, asking for admission, only to be taunted and get thrown out.

【分析】這句話主要說明了武訓努力掙錢,想上學讀書的強烈願望的破滅。原句對故事發生的時間和進入私塾的描寫頗為籠統,這是漢語的一大特點,但是,在英譯文中要詳細說明,時間:One day, 首次進入私塾的情景:asking for admission, only to be taunted and get thrown out。"富家子弟"一詞在譯文中刪去了,因為這個說法不確切。把武訓趕出校門的可能還包括富家子弟的家長和私塾先生。

意群(4)

生活的遭遇使他深感窮人不識字便沒有出路。於是,成年後,武訓開始乞討興辦義學。為了讓窮孩子能夠讀書,

Believing that poor people will never have a chance in life unless they learn to read and write, he starts a school offering free education to children of poor families.

【分析】當武訓想上學讀書的夢想破滅之後,他下決心為窮苦孩子辦義學。這一段話描述了武訓辦義學的思想基礎。至於用什麼方式,則屬於下一個意群,所以"乞討"二字在英譯文中沒有提及。"生活的遭遇"的所指也較為籠統,於是省略未譯。

意群(5)

他裝瘋賣傻三十年,每天在街上唱歌賣藝,甚至為了討錢,任人驅打。

For funds, he depends on the handouts he earns by singing foolishly comic songs and offering himself for physical abuse. He does that for as long as thirty years.

【分析】這段話是全篇最主要的部分,描述了武訓在三十年中,為了辦義學受盡了折磨和屈辱,過著非人的生活。"他裝瘋賣傻三十年"必須另起一句:He does that for as long as thirty years,以突出他受苦的時間漫長。

意群(6)

他不知道自己的義舉能否真正改變社會。他只能告訴孩子們"將來長大了,千

萬不要忘記咱們莊稼人！"

He does not know that the poor cannot improve their lot without a change of the society; all he does is to keep telling the children, "Never turn your back to the poor folk when you grow up."

【分析】這段話是整個段落的總結。"他不知道自己的義舉能否真正改變社會"是作者的話，因為武訓從來沒有打算"改變社會"，因此在譯文中必須變通，譯為 He does not know that the poor cannot improve their lot without a change of the society。

2. 詞匯選擇

篇章翻譯的最後一道工序是選詞，即詞句推敲。選詞必須在有上下文的情況下，也就是在搭建好了框架之後才能進行。請看本段翻譯中主要詞匯的選擇：

1) 乞討——說到"乞討"，我們很容易想到 beg，但是 beg 的意思很廣，也比較籠統，故而譯作 panhandling，強調乞丐的行為。例如：

· We saw several people **panhandling** in the street.

· She **panhandled** nickels and dimes from passengers in the tube.

2) 攢錢——scrape money 表示武訓 only earns enough money to provide himself with food，表現他攢錢的艱難。

3) 裝瘋賣傻，唱歌賣藝，任人驅打——這句話不能按照字面上的意思直譯：He pretends to be mad and foolish, sings songs and even allows himself to be beaten in order to get money. 如果這樣翻譯，譯文讀者不會理解其中的含義。這句話有很強的文化特色，描繪了舊中國窮苦人迫不得已的謀生手段，就連現在中國的年輕人都很難想象這番情景，更何況外國讀者呢。所以譯為：He depends on the handouts he earns by singing foolishly comic songs and offering himself for physical abuse. 這樣翻譯帶有解釋說明的成分。**abuse** 意為 to treat someone badly，例如：In this village, people are really unfriendly and **verbally abuse** outsiders all the time. 這個村的村民很欺生，對外來人常常惡語相加。

4) "千萬不要忘記咱們莊稼人！"——這句話中的"忘記"並不是 forget，而是指 to avoid or reject, or to turn a cold shoulder to somebody，"莊稼人"也不是 peasants，而是泛指窮苦人。所以翻譯成：Never turn your back to the poor folk when you grow up。

》例文二

溫哥華的居民

原文：

●溫哥華的輝煌是溫哥華人智慧和勤奮的結晶,其中包括多民族的貢獻。●加拿大地廣人稀,國土面積比中國還大,人口卻不足 3000 萬。吸收外來移民,是加拿大長期奉行的國策。●可以說,加拿大除了印第安人外,無一不是外來移民,不同的是時間長短而已。●溫哥華則更是世界上屈指可數的多民族城市。現今 180 萬溫哥華的居民中,有一半不是在本地出生的,每四個居民中,就有一個是亞洲人。●而 25 萬華人對溫哥華的經濟發展起著巨大作用,其中有一半是近十年來到溫哥華地區的,使溫哥華成為亞洲以外最大的中國人聚居地。

譯文：

Vancouver

Vancouver owes its prosperity to its immigrants as well as the indigenous population. As Canada is a thinly populated country of fewer than 30 million people living in an area larger than China in size, attracting immigrants is the country's long-standing policy. It is not exaggerating to say that all Canadians except the native Indians are foreign born with varying lengths of residence in the country. Take Vancouver. Up to half of its 1,800,000 residents are non-natives, and for very four of them, there is one Asian, making Vancouver one of the few cities in the world with a huge ethnic community. And with the 250,000 Chinese immigrants, half of whom came to the city at different times as recent as the last ten years, who are credited with the success of the city's new economy, Vancouver now boasts a Chinese community larger than in any other country outside Asia.

這一段話簡單介紹了溫哥華的人口結構,主題為:"溫哥華是亞洲以外最大的中國人聚居地"。整個段落包含五個意群,劃分方法是由文章從籠統到細節、循序漸進的敘述方式所決定的。請看詳細分析:

1. 意群切分

意群(1)

溫哥華的輝煌是溫哥華人智慧和勤奮的結晶,其中包括多民族的貢獻。

Vancouver owes its prosperity to its immigrants as well as the indigenous population.

【分析】這是一個引導句(lead),或叫主題句,點明了整個段落的主題:多民族的貢獻。

意群(2)

加拿大地廣人稀,國土面積比中國還大,人口卻不足 3000 萬。吸收外來移民,是加拿大長期奉行的國策。

As Canada is a thinly populated country of fewer than 30 million people living in an area larger than China in size, attracting immigrants is the country's long-standing policy.

【分析】這段話是主題句的論據,主要說明溫哥華成為一個移民城市的原因: "吸收外來移民,是加拿大長期奉行的國策。"而"加拿大地廣人稀,國土面積比中國還大,人口卻不足 3000 萬。"又是吸收外來移民國策的客觀原因,所以要用 **as** 引導的從句。

意群(3)

可以說,加拿大除了印第安人外,無一不是外來移民,不同的是時間長短而已。

It is not exaggerating to say that all Canadians except the native Indians are foreign born with varying lengths of residence in the country.

【分析】此句用來強調為什麼說加拿大是個移民國家,因為只有印第安人才是加拿大的原住民。這又是一個過渡句,引出主題"溫哥華的居民"。

意群(4)

溫哥華則更是世界上屈指可數的多民族城市。現今 180 萬溫哥華的居民中,有一半不是在本地出生的,每四個居民中,就有一個是亞洲人。

Take Vancouver. Up to half of its 1,800,000 residents are non-natives, and for very four of them, there is one Asian, making Vancouver one of the few cities in the world with a huge ethnic community.

【分析】這段話仍是一個過渡句,進一步說明"溫哥華的居民大部分是亞洲人"。

意群(5)

而25萬華人對溫哥華的經濟發展起著巨大作用,其中有一半是近十年來到溫哥華地區的,使溫哥華成為亞洲以外最大的中國人聚居地。

And with the 250,000 Chinese immigrants, half of whom came to the city at different times as recent as the last ten years, who are credited with the success of the city's new economy, Vancouver now boasts a Chinese community larger than in any other country outside Asia.

【分析】經過四個意群層層深入的敘述,最後點明主題:溫哥華是亞洲以外最大的中國人聚居地。這個段落原文條理比較清楚,切分意群並不太難。但是,在選詞方面仍有一定的難度。

2. 詞彙選擇

1)**溫哥華的輝煌是溫哥華人智慧和勤奮的結晶**——這是漢語中常用的套語(cliché),在漢語的上下文中也許很正常,但在英語中卻不常見。其中"輝煌、智慧、勤奮、結晶"負載的信息過多,都不能按照字面意思直譯,不能想當然地譯做 glory, wisdom, diligence, crystallization,因為在英譯文的語境裡,這些單詞並不表示那些意思。這裡的"輝煌"其實是"繁榮"的意思,"結晶"應理解為"歸功於",譯做 owe 比較合適,owe 的意思就是 as a result, because of。例如:

· I *owe* my success to my teachers.

· He *owes* his life to the doctors and nurses at the hospital.

整句話譯成 Vancouver owes its prosperity to its immigrants as well as the indigenous population,很恰當。

2)**25萬華人對溫哥華的經濟發展起著巨大作用**——原文中沒有點清楚這個結論是誰下的,但在譯文中要說明:人們都這樣認為,所以要用被動式短語 be credited with,意思是 to consider (someone) as (having good qualities or having done something good),例如:

· The teacher has always *been credited with* understanding and sympathy for his students.

· He *is often credited with* originating political reform in this country.

3)**溫哥華成為亞洲以外最大的中國人聚居地**——這里的"成為"不僅是 become，其中暗含著一種自豪感，所以要用 boast，意為 to have or possess（something to be proud of），例如：

· This city **boasts** beautiful beaches, great restaurants and friendly locals.
· Beijing **boasts** many historical places and modern flyovers.

≫ 例文三

我的母親

●在我們家里，母親是至高無上的守護神。日常生活全是母親料理。三餐飯菜，四季衣裳，孩子的教養，親友的聯繫，需要多少精力！●我自幼多病，常在和病魔作鬥爭。能夠不斷戰勝疾病的主要原因是我的母親。如果沒有母親，很難想象我會活下來。●在昆明時嚴重貧血，站著站著就暈倒。●後來索性染上肺結核休學在家。當時的治法是一天吃五個雞蛋，曬半小時太陽。母親特地把我的床安排在有陽光的地方，無論多忙，這半小時必在我身邊，一分鐘也不能少。●我曾由於各種原因多次發高燒，除延醫服藥外，母親費盡精神護理。用小匙喂水，用涼手巾敷在額上。●有一次高燒昏迷中，覺得像是在一個狹窄的洞中穿行，擠不過去，我以為自己就要死了，一抓到母親的手，立刻知道我是在家里，我是平安的。●後來我經歷了名目繁多的手術，人贈雅號"挨千刀的"。在挨千刀的過程中，也是母親，一次又一次陪我奔走醫院，醫院的人以為是我陪母親，其實是母親陪我。●我過了40歲，還是覺得睡在母親身邊最心安。

——宗璞：《花朝節的紀念》

譯文：

Mother And I

If there was a center in our family life, it was my mother. We depended on her for our daily meals, for all the clothes we wore, for the education of the offsprings and the maintenance of contact with our friends and relatives. Just imagine the strain all those duties subjected her to.

From childhood on, I suffered from one disease after another. It was mainly my mother who, with her meticulous care she took of me, helped me survive all the misfortunes. When we were in Kunming, I was down with serious anemia. It was so bad that I could hardly stand on my feet or I would pass out. To make things worse, I later developed TB and had to quit school. The usual treatment for this disease that I received was primitive: daily consumption of five eggs and a half-hour session of sunning. So my mother moved my bed to a sunny corner in the house. For each sunning session, she would drop whatever she was doing and stay with me for a full half hour.

As I lay recuperating, I was stricken with high fever many times for various causes. When that happened, in addition to the doctor's attendance, I had my mother taking such care of me as a devoted nurse would, feeding me water spoon by spoon, keeping changing damp cool towels on my forehead, and attending to all the other things she thought needed to be done for me. Once in a delirium, I had the hallucination that I was squeezing my way in a narrow tunnel with difficulty, and just when I began to tremble with the fear of death, I felt the hands of my mother; immediately I knew I was home and safe.

From then on I underwent a series of surgical operations, so many that I became jocularly known as "The Stabs". Each time I was hospitalized, mother would be with me. As she was always seen keeping me company, those in the hospitals would mistake my mother for the patient, and me her attendant. I am now in my forties, but it still gives me a sense of security to sleep next to her.

這是一篇回憶錄的節選,追憶了母親對兒女無微不至的關懷。布局合理,敘述比較完整,按照內容切分意群並不太難,但是,受漢語意合模式的影響,本段仍有幾處寫得語焉不詳,這使得翻譯時很難把意群有效地連接起來,要選擇合適恰當的詞彙就更難。整個段落可分為 8 個意群,每個意群之間的連接必須自然連貫,選詞必須精準達意,現綜合起來進行分析。

意群(1)

在我們家裡,母親是至高無上的守護神。日常生活全是母親料理。三餐飯菜,四季衣裳,孩子的教養,親友的聯繫,需要多少精力!

If there was *a center* in our family life, it was my mother. **We depended on her for** our daily meals, for all the clothes we wore, for the education of the offsprings and the maintenance of contact with our friends and relatives. Just imagine the strain all those duties subjected her to.

【分析】這句話是中國式寫作模式中常見的"總帽",起著統領全篇的作用。但是,"至高無上的守護神"卻與下面的例子不相符,因為"三餐飯菜,四季衣裳,孩子的教養,親友的聯繫"不應是一個"守護神"辦的事,本文裡的"守護神"其實就是一種比喻,但在英語里卻沒有相對的說法,所以這里譯成 a center 和 We depended on her for...。此處連用了三個介詞 for,是很符合英語常用介詞的講話習慣的。

意群(2)

我自幼多病,常在和病魔作鬥爭。能夠不斷戰勝疾病的主要原因是我的母親。如果沒有母親,很難想象我會活下來。

From childhood on, I suffered from one disease after another. It was mainly my mother who, with her meticulous care she took of me, helped me survive all the misfortunes.

【分析】這里的"常在和病魔作鬥爭"是典型的中國式比喻,幾乎成了 cliché,這種比喻不符合英語習慣,所以譯成 I suffered from one disease after another。

意群(3)

在昆明時嚴重貧血,站著站著就暈倒。

When we were in Kunming, I was down with serious anemia. It was so bad that I could hardly stand on my feet or I would pass out.

【分析】這里的"站著站著就暈倒"必須先釋義,後翻譯,換句話說就是"幾乎站不了多久,站得時間長了就會暈倒"。所以翻成 I could hardly stand on my feet or I would pass out。

意群(4)

後來索性染上肺結核休學在家。當時的治法是一天吃五個雞蛋,曬半小時太陽。母親特地把我的床安排在有陽光的地方,無論多忙,這半小時必在我身邊,一分鐘也不能少。

To make things worse, I later developed TB and had to quit school. *The usual treatment for this disease that I received was primitive*: daily consumption of five eggs and a half-hour session of sunning. So my mother moved my bed to a sunny corner in the house. For each sunning session, she would drop whatever she was doing and stay with me for a full half hour.

【分析】這句話中的"當時的治法"暗指"在當時醫學不發達時給作者治病用的、非常落後的偏方",漢語原文雖未明說,但英譯文必須講清楚,所以譯為 The usual treatment for this disease that I received was primitive。

意群(5)

我曾由於各種原因多次發高燒,除延醫服藥外,母親費盡精神護理。用小匙喂水,用涼手巾覆在額上。

As I lay recuperating, I was stricken with high fever many times for various causes. When that happened, in addition to the doctor's attendance, *I had my mother taking such care of me as a devoted nurse would*, *feeding me water spoon by spoon*, *keeping changing damp cool towels on my forehead*, *and all the other things she thought needed to be done for me.*

【分析】這一段是意群(4)的繼續,漢語原文沒有明顯的連接方式,但英語必須加上段落過渡連接詞語:As I lay recuperating。另外,"母親費盡精神護理"是漢語常用套話,幾乎是 cliché,如果直譯,會顯得感情不充分,所以譯成 I had my mother taking such care of me *as a devoted nurse would*。"用小匙喂水,用涼手巾覆在額上"敘述也太平淡,因為做母親的都會這樣做,因此英譯文必須敘述細節:feeding me water spoon by spoon, keeping changing damp cool towels on my forehead。除了"用小匙喂水,用涼手巾覆在額上"以外,一個母親為了照顧生病的孩子,還要做很多事情,這裡都"盡在不言中"了,英譯文中必須加上:and attending to all the other things she thought needed to be done for me。

意群(6)

有一次高燒昏迷中,覺得像是在一個狹窄的洞中穿行,擠不過去,我以為自己就要死了,一抓到母親的手,立刻知道我是在家裡,我是平安的。

Once in a *delirium*, I had the *hallucination* that I was squeezing my way in a narrow tunnel with difficulty, and just when *I began to tremble with the fear of death*, I felt the hands of my mother; immediately I knew I was home and safe.

【分析】這一段中的"高燒昏迷"屬於用詞不當,因為如果人昏迷了,就沒有知覺了,也就沒有下文的幻覺了。這裡的"昏迷"應該是"精神錯亂",英語要譯作 delirium,下面的"幻覺",漢語中沒有,英譯文也要加以說明:I had the hallucination…。**"我以為自己就要死了"**,如果直譯也會顯得平淡無力,因此譯作 I began to tremble with the fear of death,以加強語氣。

意群(7)

後來我經歷了名目繁多的手術,人贈雅號"挨千刀的"。在挨千刀的過程中,也是母親,一次又一次陪我奔走醫院,醫院的人以為是我陪母親,其實是母親陪我。

From then on I underwent a series of surgical operations, so many that I became jocularly known as "The Stabs". Each time I was hospitalized, mother would be with me. As she was always seen keeping me company, those in the hospitals would mistake my mother for the patient, and me her attendant.

【分析】這里的"人贈雅號'挨千刀的'"是一句諧謔語,其中包含了中國人在交際中常用的玩笑話,因為"挨千刀的"還是一句罵人的話,這層意思無法再現於英譯文,只能用 The Stabs 對之。

意群(8)

我過了 40 歲,還是覺得睡在母親身邊最心安。

I am now in my forties, but it still gives me a sense of security to sleep next to her.

【分析】本段最後一句話講得很感人,但漢語中的"過了 40 歲"時態不甚明確,可能是作者寫這篇回憶錄的時候,也可能是以前的某個時期,在英譯文中用現在時,比較生動。

通過上述三個譯例,我們可以看出篇章翻譯的整個過程必須分為閱讀全文、意群分切和選詞組句三個步驟,即使是資深翻譯家,也不能一拿到材料,就動手翻譯,更不能草草一看便對文本內容心領神會,然後揮筆而就。實踐證明,越是資深的翻譯家,就越講究反覆琢磨原文,仔細推敲詞義。因為翻譯不同於創作,譯作必須在忠實於原作的框架內發揮選詞造句的創造性。沒有"**閱讀全文──意群分切──選詞組句**"這"三部曲",便沒有好的譯文。

思考題

1. 在篇章翻譯中,採取"閱讀全文──意群分切──選詞組句"的三個步驟的原因是什麼?
2. 意群分切和選詞的主要依據是什麼?

第十五章　原文中文字的合理刪減

在所譯文本中,經常出現與主題無關的內容或文字,稱為"冗餘成分" (deadwood)。對這些多餘的內容,在確保忠實於原文中心意思和主要內容的情況下,譯者有權進行必要的刪減。可以刪減的內容包括:沒有實際意義的常用套話、與內容無關的掌故或俗話、只在漢語環境中有意義但沒必要對英譯文讀者解釋的事物,以及表述混亂或詞不達意的內容。在上述情況下,譯者有責任刪減冗餘、修正謬誤、彌補不足。正如美國作家 E. B. White 在主張簡潔明了的寫作風格時所做的論述:

A sentence should contain no unnecessary words, a paragraph no unnecessary sentences, for the same reason that a drawing should have no unnecessary lines and machine no unnecessary parts. This requires not that the writer make all his sentence short or that he avoid all detail... but every word tell.

(李觀儀,2004:140)

這個論斷也適用於翻譯,對那些可有可無的成分,一律刪去,毫不可惜,以使所保留的每個詞與句子充分發揮應有的作用(to make every word tell)。下面請看譯例分析:

一、刪減套話

在漢語交際中常常出現約定俗成的套語,例如:"封建迷信"、"黨的教育事業"、"安全隱患"等。其中的"封建"、"黨的……事業"、"安全"都是多餘的,不必翻譯。這些詞語可分別譯為:superstition, education, hidden trouble 即可。篇章翻譯也是如此,在很多文章中,開頭總少不了一個"總帽",缺了這個"帽",好像文章開頭會顯得突兀。例如,我們總能從"總帽"中預測新聞內容:一聽到"一方有難,

八方支援",就知道發生了災難。請看下列譯例:

≫ 例文一

未來廣播電視的發展與管理系統

(論文提要)

原文:

　　人類即將進入21世紀,中國的廣播電視事業取得了迅猛發展。在這千年轉換,世紀之交的歷史時刻,回顧過去,業績輝煌;展望未來,前程似錦。

　　本文主要討論21世紀中國廣播電視發展的趨勢與系統管理等問題。文章分為四大部分:

　　第一部分:總結了中國廣播電視在發展過程中存在的十大矛盾;

　　第二部分:提出了21世紀我國廣播電視將面臨的挑戰;

　　第三部分:概括歸納了未來我國廣播電視的發展趨向;

　　第四部分:探討了如何運用現代管理理論與方法及現代管理手段,加強廣播電視交流等問題。

　　【分析】論文提要的語言特點就是簡明扼要,但這篇論文提要的頭一段話就是典型的"總帽",沒有必要翻譯。譯文應當"開門見山",只說要點:

譯文:

ABSTRACT

Prospects for the Systematic Administration
of China's Radio and TV Broadcasting

This paper covers the trend in China's radio and TV broadcasting development and important issues in the systematic administration of this field.

The paper consists of four parts: Part One is a summary of ten dichotomies which arose during the development of China's radio and TV broadcasting. Part Two outlines the challenges China may face in the future. In Part Three, the writer predicts tendencies for China's broadcasting. Part Four contains an analysis of the way modern administrative theories, methods and techniques should be used to strengthen the systematic administration of China's radio and TV broadcasting.

》》 例文二

女性獨身現象

原文：

獨身女性常常**把感情寄托在工作或者業餘愛好上**，和有家庭的人相比，她們的生活倒也輕鬆、寧靜。**很多大齡女性都希望有一個自己的小天地，安安靜靜地生活，做點自己想做的事情。**

獨身女性生活雖然無拘無束、自由自在，但是在我們國家，由於經濟條件和傳統觀念的影響，**獨身女性在社會上的處境還是比較艱難的。**她們遇到的最大的一個問題是**周圍人的不理解**，女性到了30歲以後還沒有結婚，周圍的人往往會說長道短，有的人會猜測，獨身女性不是有生理缺陷就是**心理變態**，再不就是可能與某個有婦之夫搞婚外戀。還有的人以嘲笑的態度看待獨身女性，說她們"**沒人要，剩下了，嫁不出去了**"。種種無端的懷疑、猜測和嘲諷給獨身女性增加了很多精神上的壓力，**使她們本來就孤獨寂寞的心受到了更大的傷害。**

譯文：

Single Women in China

Single women often pour their energies into their careers or hobbies. Compared with some married women, their life is more relaxed and peaceful. But even so, single women in China have their own special problems because of the current economic situation and as a result of the persistence of traditional ways of thinking.

One of their problems is that people gossip about them. In China, single middle-aged women are often the subject of wild speculation. Some people jump to the conclusion that there must be something wrong physiologically with them or that they don't like men or they must be involved with married men. Some ridicule them saying that these women have been left "on the shelf". All this idle gossip causes much pressure and stress, and adds salt to the wound of not finding a mate.

【分析】這是一篇電臺廣播稿節選，評論中國女性獨身現象，里面充滿了中國人常用的表達方式，已成俗套。這些俗套是不能詞對詞、句對句地直譯成英語的。具體分析如下：

1）**把感情寄托在工作或者業餘愛好上**——中國人講這句話無可厚非，但講英語的人認為人只能把"感情"（emotion）寄托在親人或子女身上，但不能寄托在工作或業餘愛好上。因此只能譯作 Single women often pour their *energies* into their careers or hobbies，即："把精力放在工作或業餘愛好上"。

2）**很多大齡女性都希望有一個自己的小天地，安安靜靜地生活，做點自己想做的事情**——這句話聽起來並不錯，但仔細推敲起來，句中所說的是不言自明的事（truism），也可以說是一句廢話，誰不想"有一個自己的小天地，安安靜靜地生活，做點自己想做的事情"呢？故刪去不譯。

3）**獨身女性在社會上的處境還是比較艱難的，周圍人的不理解**——中國人總是把"社會"、"處境"、"理解"等詞放在嘴邊，例如，學生畢業時找工作叫"走向社會"，丈夫在家受氣叫"家庭處境糟糕"。英語中這些詞的使用要少得多，所以英譯文中只能譯作 Single women in China have their own special problems。"周圍人的不理解"乾脆刪去不譯。

4）**心理變態**——如果把這個詞當作醫學名詞，可以直譯為 psychopathology，但是這樣譯專業性太強，原文中的意思只不過是"對男人不感興趣"，可以譯作 they don't like men。

5）**沒人要，剩下了，嫁不出去**——原文表示很多人有此議論，但是都譯成英語便是重複，可以只譯作 left on the shelf 這一習慣用語，例如：In those days，if you hadn't married by the time you were 30，you were definitely *on the shelf*。

6）**使她們本來就孤獨寂寞的心受到了更大的傷害**——這也是典型的中國式表達法，直譯不符合英語習慣，也過於籠統，所以只能意譯為 adds salt to the wound of not finding a mate。

二、縮減中式表達方式

》 例文三

農民收藏家

陳孝榮

原文：

我的家鄉雲南有一個農民，過去是縣屬國營酒廠的職工，因企業不景氣被"**精簡**"回了鄉。可這個農民是個小個子，才一米五幾，**不適合在大山裡生存**。他只好背著一個老式 120 相機走村串寨給人照相混口飯吃。

可那時農民窮得很,沒人舍得花錢照什麼相。**那農民的腦子很活**,說照相不給錢也行,給點他們用不著的老家具、舊衣服就可以。這樣的交換條件,村民自然**樂不可支**,因為**那些舊東西早不時興了,擺在家里還占地方。**

那農民從此就干起了文物收藏。那時的山里人誰也不知道這就叫文物收藏,他們都把那農民叫做"怪物"、"傻子"、"不務正業的人"。就連他妻子也是如此,見到家里的破爛越來越多,沒少跟他大吵大鬧,為這夫妻倆差點離了婚。

後來我們縣大辦旅遊,**他的機遇來了**。聽說有個少數民族文物收藏家,來他家參觀的人絡繹不絕,**他一下子就出了名。省市縣鎮幾級領導高度重視**,撥出專款讓他把那個雞籠似的小屋換成了寬敞明亮的平房。

——《衛生與生活》周刊,2006-1-2

譯文:

From Junk to Cultural Artifacts

This is a story of how a laid-off factory worker became a well-known collector of cultural artifacts.

When he left the factory, a bankrupt state-run brewery in the city, this man went back to his home village in the mountainous Yunnan Province. But he was physically unfit for farm work in the mountains, being only a little over 1.5m in height. To eke out a living, he became a traveling photographer with an old camera, going from house to house, looking for customers.

He didn't have much luck. Having their pictures taken was a luxury the farmers could not afford. But that did not stop him. He told them that if they didn't have the money to pay him, he would accept for his service whatever they could give him such as run-down furniture or clothes that they had no use for and wanted to get rid of. It worked. The farmers took his offer as a windfall, thinking he must be an eccentric, a fool or trash. And his wife, who hated what he was doing, would from time to time throw a tantrum, even threaten divorce, over the ever-expanding piles of junk her husband collected. They did not know that the throwaways could be of cultural value.

A few years later, life began to smile at him. With tourism becoming a booming industry in the county, he became known as a collector of ethnic cultural artifacts. Legions of visitors flocked to his home, and when the local authorities learned of this, they had his chicken-coop-like shanty converted into a shining, spacious one-story house.

【分析】這是一篇介紹中國改革開放初期的傳奇人物的文章,重點是他如何從一個收破爛的成為民俗收藏家的過程。漢語原文比較囉嗦,冗餘成分很多,英譯時必須做必要的刪減。

1) **我的家鄉雲南有一個農民,過去是縣屬國營酒廠的職工,因企業不景氣被"精簡"回了鄉。**——這是典型的漢語敘事方式,像說書一樣:"一切從頭說起……"。英譯文讀者關心的是事情的經過和結果,其他細節並不重要,沒有必要翻譯。一句引導語就足夠了:This is a story of how a laid-off factory worker became a well-known collector of cultural artifacts。

2) **那農民的腦子很活,村民自然樂不可支。**——這是典型的中文表達方式,英譯必須變通:The farmers took his offer as a windfall。windfall 是人們得到了"沒想到的好事",表示"驚奇"。

3) **那些舊東西早不時興了,擺在家里還占地方。**——這是老百姓的慣用語,指的是"破爛兒",譯成 something that they had no use for and wanted to get rid of 即可。

4) **他的機遇來了**——這句話也是套話,不能直譯為 His opportunity has come,應該譯作 life began to smile at him,意指"他時來運轉了"。

5) **省市縣鎮幾級領導高度重視**——中國人言必稱"各級領導高度重視",是典型的套話,沒必要譯成 leaders at various levels,譯為 the local authorities 即可。

三、刪減重複

漢語習慣於重複詞語,有時是為了強調所要表達的意思,增添文採,給對方留下深刻的印象;有時是為了促成結構的整齊、勻稱。保持結構的均衡反應了中國人的美學心理。必要的重複不但不顯冗贅,反而增添了情趣,突出了主題,給人以美感和流暢感。

而英語總的傾向是盡量避免重複。講英語的人對隨意重複相同的詞語或句式往往感到厭煩。"在能明確表達意思的前提下,英語宜盡量採用替代、省略或變換等方式來避免無意圖的(unintentional)重複。這樣不僅能使行文簡潔、有力,而且比較符合英語民族的語言心理習慣"(連淑能,1993:176)。這樣一來,漢英翻譯就遇到了矛盾。本著以譯文讀者的語言習慣和接受傾向為主的原則,譯者必須進行必要的結構轉換:化繁為簡、刪去冗贅。

例如：

· 你**不願意落後**，他也**不願意落後**，誰都**不願意落後**。

You don't want to lag behind. ***Neither does*** he or anybody else.

· 他們犯過**錯誤**，吃過**錯誤**的虧，也承認**錯誤**，研究**錯誤**，但關鍵是要牢記**錯誤**，從錯誤中吸取教訓。

They made mistakes, suffered by ***them***, acknowledged and studied ***them***, but they must never forget ***them*** so that they can learn their lessons.

· 我們**談到**了自己，**談到**前途，**談到**幸福，**談到**學習，**談到**彼此的情況——談到一切，就是沒有**談到**當時的政局。

We talked of ourselves, ***of*** our prospects, ***of*** happiness, ***of*** study, ***of*** each other—***of*** everything but the political situation then.

· 我們這一代人經歷了各種各樣的**災難**，有三年的"自然**災難**"，有十年動亂的政治**災難**，還有目前物欲橫流的社會**災難**。

Our generation has experienced various ***disasters***, such as " the three-year ***famine***"(1959–1961), the ten-year ***catastrophe***(1966–1976) and the trend of ***excessive desire*** for material comfort now.

請看以下實例：

》》 例文四

拒　絕

（節選）

原文：

朋友家里都裝了空調，**老王不要**，他說："人本來是能適應氣溫變化的，裝上空調，人的適應能力自然就退化了，人越活越嬌氣，有什麼好！"

　　朋友都購置了電腦，**老王不要**，他說："在我還沒得老年痴呆症以前，我的人腦已經夠用了，要電腦做什麼？用上電腦，人就變成電腦的奴隸了。"

　　朋友都購置了移動電話，**老王不要**，他說："只有最淺薄的小暴發戶才弄個移動電話耍耍，連歐洲的後現代名家都說了，移動電話是為了搞破鞋的男人和逃稅的走私者準備的，你們看看，副部長以上和副教授以上的人物誰提著個移動電話？"

　　朋友都買了電視機，**老王不要**，他說："大量論證告訴我們，**看電視就是接受精神控制，就是人的主體性的喪失**，就是吸精神鴉片，我才不要那玩意兒呢。"

　　朋友談起來，都說老王**很偉大**。

過了幾年,大家發現,老王家里有了空調,有了電視機,有了移動與不移動的電話,有了一切能導致"精神危機"的產品。老王說:"這些東西越好用,我的精神危機就越嚴重。有了電腦,就有幸福嗎? 有了電視,就有愛情嗎? 有了空調,就有友誼嗎? 有了小康,就有和睦家庭嗎? 有了現代化,就有真理、正義、公平和高尚嗎? 我確實討厭這些東西,但我還是用了這些東西,這難道不是人類的悲劇嗎? 難道我們是為了一些花花哨哨的小玩意兒才來到這個世界上的嗎? "

於是大家覺得老王**不但偉大而且深刻**,覺得老王是本世紀最深刻的人之一。

——王蒙:《尷尬風流》

譯文:

Refusing to Follow the Trend

Mr. Wang is old-fashioned in his ways. He seems to like nothing modern. When air conditioners became commonplace in China, he refused to have one installed in his house, saying that the conditioner would take away your adaptability to changes in the weather and make you weaker.

When the personal computer was all the rage, Mr. Wang refused to get one, saying that he's not an Alzheimer's case and his mind functioned quite well, and he didn't want to be a slave to the "electronic brain".

When mobile phones became a status symbol, he gave a snort of contempt at them, saying that they're for garish upstarts only. And if you see one with a cell phone, you may be sure that the guy is a womanizer, smuggler or tax evader. You don't see anyone above the rank of vice minister or associate professor walk around with a cell phone in his hand. Mr. Wang went so far as to call television "spiritual opium", saying that you would let yourself be led by the nose by what you saw on television. So all his friends called Mr. Wang weird.

A few years later, people found Mr. Wang acquired all those things he had hated: an air-conditioner, a TV and a mobile phone, things that make life meaningless. He said, "Yes, these things make life easier for me, but I feel bored because of them. They don't give me love, friendship or happiness. I hate them, but I need them. Isn't it sad?" For this people began to view Mr. Wang with higher regard, saying that he was the greatest thinker of this century.

【分析】這是一篇帶有嘲諷性質的散文節選,描繪了社會上的兩種人:一種是緊追時髦,什麼先進,就用什麼;另一種是墨守傳統,任何時髦的東西都不屑一顧。文中運用了一些重複手段,強調了主人公不隨波逐流的性格。下面做簡略分析:

1)**朋友……,老王不要,他說:**——這個句型重複了四遍,以突出"老王"事事與眾不同。雖然多次重複,但中文讀者並不覺得厭煩,反而覺得饒有趣味。如果英語也採取這樣的句型,譯成 All his friends have bought... but Mr. Wang refused to...,就不符合英語有意識地避免重複的表達習慣了。為此,英譯文採用了四種不同的說法:

When air conditioners ***became commonplace*** in China, he refused to have one installed in his house, saying...

When the personal computer ***was all the rage***, Mr. Wang refused to get one, saying...

When mobile phones ***became a status symbol***, he gave a snort of contempt at them, saying...

Mr. Wang went so far as to call television "spiritual opium", saying...

雖然漢語原文中沒有一一對應的文字,但字里行間都暗含了同樣的意思。

became commonplace(成為普通用品);was all the rage(風靡一時);became a status symbol(成為社會地位的象徵),Mr. Wang went so far as to call television...(老王做事太過分了,竟然把電視叫做……)

2)**看電視就是接受精神控制,就是人的主體性的喪失**——這是目前流行的、非常典型的籠統說法,看似源自英語,實為中國人自造。英譯文必須明確表達:You would let yourself be led by the nose by what you saw on television。下面這句話也是如此:**老王家里……有了一切能導致精神危機的產品**——Mr. Wang acquired all those things he had hated... things that make life meaningless.

3)**都說老王很偉大**——這里的"偉大",帶有諷刺意味,是指"古怪"(weird)。後面的"**深刻**"也是同理,因此用 the greatest thinker 對之。

4)**"這些東西越好用,我的精神危機就越嚴重。有了電腦,就有幸福嗎?有了電視,就有愛情嗎?有了空調,就有友誼嗎?有了小康,就有和睦家庭嗎?有了現代化,就有真理、正義、公平和高尚嗎?我確實討厭這些東西,但我還是用了這些東西,這難道不是人類的悲劇嗎?難道我們是為了一些花花哨哨的小玩意兒才來到這個世界上的嗎?"**—— 這段話很松散、囉嗦,沒有什麼邏輯性,因此英譯文要做必要的刪減,使之簡單明了:

"Yes, these things make life easier for me, but I feel bored because of them. They don't give me love, friendship or happiness. I hate them, but I need them. Isn't it sad?"

　　以上譯例是比較典型的需要進行刪減的文本節選,在翻譯實踐中遇到的情況也許會很難察覺。這就需要譯者不斷分析漢英兩種語言在修辭和句型方面的差異,從而摸索出規律來。

思考題

1. 為什麼要對漢語原文的文字進行刪減? 刪減的依據是什麼?
2. 對原文的刪減是否會有損於原文的內容或文採?

第十六章　釋義性翻譯

　　漢英兩種語言中都有很多詞句具有濃鬱的民族文化特徵,如果按照字面意思翻譯,不僅不能達意,反而會引起讀者誤解。對於這種情況,只能採用釋義性翻譯法(paraphrase)。對於這一點,Eugene Nida 說得好:

In fact, all translating involves differing degrees of paraphrasing, since there is no way in which one can translate successfully word for word and structure for structure. ...

Since languages do not differ essentially in what they can say, but how they say it, paraphrase is inevitable. What is important is the semantic legitimacy of the paraphrase.

　　當然,釋義並不是隨意解釋,而是要盡量運用譯文讀者的習慣用法來代替他們無法理解或理解有困難的詞句,以便他們盡量透徹地理解原文。釋義法的關鍵是譯文的修辭要合理(semantic legitimacy),這種方法在英漢翻譯中較為突出,例如:

Not long ago I heard myself describe a friend, half-jokingly, as "a much better person than I am, that is, she doesn't gossip so much." I heard my voice *distorted by that same false note that sometimes creeps into it when social strain and some misguided notion of amiability make me assent to opinions I don't really share.*

——Francine Prose, *Gossip*

　　這段話的粗斜體部分是無法直譯的,即便是勉強詞對詞地翻譯出來,也不能達意。因此,必須先把它用英語解釋一下再譯成中文。釋義如下:

I praised my friend saying that she doesn't gossip so much, but I found I did not speak sincerely because of the pressure from society. In fact I don't agree to the opinion that it is wrong to gossip. I made that untruthful statement just to please my friend.

釋義性譯文：

不久前,我無意中半開玩笑似地稱讚一個朋友,說她"比我強多了,因為她不大在背後議論人。"說這話時,我覺得我的語調不正常,因為言不由衷。這種情況時有發生,因為出於禮貌,出於對謙和的誤解,所以對別人的看法儘管不同意,我也隨聲附和。

再看一例：

Some Americans are extremely overweight. **The condition is costly.** Doctor Koop says $ 70,000,000,000 are spent each year to treat diseases related to being overweight. **The condition can be deadly**, **too.** Each year, 300,000 overweight Americans die before reaching old age.

這一段中的兩句話:The condition is costly 和 The condition can be deadly, too. 是無法直譯的,因此必須根據上下文加以解釋：

有些美國人體重過高,**因此減肥的費用就特別高。** 據庫珀博士說,每年用在醫治與肥胖有關的疾病上的錢就有 700 億美元。**而且肥胖症還會致命,** 每年約有 30 萬過於肥胖的美國人早逝。

漢英翻譯也是如此,但是作為中國人,我們往往把自己習以為常的表達方式,理所當然地認為對英譯文讀者說來也很容易理解。殊不知,詞對詞的翻譯會使他們覺得意思很模糊或聽起來很別扭。例如：

》例文一

北京站

原文：

北京站建成於 1959 年 9 月 15 日, 由毛澤東**親筆**題寫站名。她是**偉大祖國首都**的**象徵和門戶**。目前日旅客流量居全國之首,成為聯繫祖國各地的**橋梁和紐帶**。北京站人**本著**"人民鐵路為人民"的宗旨,熱情歡迎您的到來。

詞對詞直譯：

When Beijing Station was established on September 15, 1959, Chairman Mao Zedong inscribed for it *in his own handwriting*. It is *a symbol of our great motherland and a door of capital Beijing*. Recently, it has the highest flow of travelers everyday compared with other stations in China. It now plays a role as *a bridge and tie with every corner of China*. The staff in Beijing Station will always remember the principle of "*Serving the people*," *and greet every traveler warmly*.

釋義性翻譯：

The Beijing Station was completed on September 15, 1959. The new building was *honored with* the inscription of its name by Chairman Mao Zedong. A *landmark* in the capital city and *hub* of the nation's railway systems, the station tops the country's record in the number of passengers it handles daily. We at the station will give all its passengers *the best service we can offer*.

【分析】這是一篇帶有廣告性質的簡介節選，主要是向顧客介紹北京站的歷史與現狀。漢語原文中的用詞符合漢語重籠統的語言習慣，但不符合英語重具體的語言習慣，具體分析如下：

1）**親筆**題寫站名——任何人題詞都是"親筆"，否則就是"代筆"了，所以，譯成 Chairman Mao Zedong inscribed for it in his own handwriting 就很滑稽。漢語中的"親筆"實際上是要體現得到毛澤東的題詞是一種殊榮，所以譯做 was honored with the inscription of its name by Chairman Mao Zedong。

2）**偉大祖國，象徵和門戶，橋梁和紐帶**——這些詞的感情色彩過濃，而且多是比喻。英語簡介只需陳述事實，沒必要體現作者的情感，所以譯作 a landmark in the capital city and hub of the nation's railway systems。

3）**本著"人民鐵路為人民"的宗旨，熱情歡迎您的到來**——"人民鐵路為人民"是中國常見的標語口號，我們已習以為常，但是譯成英語便沒有什麼實際意義，故刪去不譯。"熱情歡迎您的到來"與整篇的內容不太銜接。整句話的實際含義是"我們盡力為顧客提供最好的服務"，譯為 We at the station will give all its passengers the best service we can offer 即可。

例文二

我的祖母

原文：

　　我的祖母是一位又有才干、又**有經驗的人，家務都由她主持**，只是**脾氣太大，約束家里人嚴厲極了**。偶犯**小過**，便遭**申斥**，家里的人沒有不怕她的，唯獨對我特別**鐘愛**，從未打過一下，罵過一句，這也是我小時候很聰慧、會**伺候**她的緣故。

——劉半農：《賽金花本事》

譯文一

　　My grandmother was a capable and *experienced* person, who *took care of all the housework*, but she was *bad-tempered* and very strict with her family. She might *scold* you for the occasional *minor mistakes* and all the family members are afraid of her. However, she *loved* me so much that she never blamed or hit me. This is because I was brilliant and *able to take care of* her.

譯文二

　　My grandmother, a capable and *worldly-wise* woman, *had absolute control in running the family*. She was a *severe and formidable disciplinarian* who would *punish* anyone in the family for the *slightest offences* they made. For that she was feared by all —all, but not me. As I was an intelligent girl and knew *how to please* her, I was *the apple of her eye.*

　　【分析】這是一篇人物傳記節選，是書中主人公對祖母的回憶，用詞非常具有漢語特點，英譯文必須根據英語習慣進行解釋，具體分析如下：

　　1) **有經驗的**——這個詞不能籠統地譯成 experienced，必須說明在哪方面"有經驗"，作者的祖母看來是個"精明、外場、善於處世"的人：experienced in the affairs of life；sophisticated；practical；having or showing prudence and shrewdness in dealing with *worldly* matters，所以要用 worldly-wise。

　　2) **家務都由她主持**——這里的"家務"並不是做飯、收拾屋子等家務事，譯文一所用的 housework 或者 household chores 都不符合原意。原文是指"管理家事"，所以用 had absolute control in running the family。

3）**脾氣太大，約束家里人嚴厲極了**——這里的"脾氣太大"不是 bad-tempered，而是"讓人敬畏的"，所以，譯文二所用的 formidable 很合適，這個詞的意思就是 causing fear, respect or great anxiety; awesome。"約束家里人嚴厲極了"譯為 severe disciplinarian，意思是 someone who believes in keeping complete control of the people she is in charge of, esp. by giving strong punishments。

4）**申斥**——不僅是 scold，而是籠統地代表各種懲罰，所以用 punish。

5）**小過**——譯文一用的是 mistakes，顯然不對，因為 mistake 的意思是：an action or opinion that is not correct, or that produces a result you did not want。這里的"小過"其實是指 an act or cause of upsetting or annoying somebody，所以用 offense 比較合適。

6）**鐘愛**——這里指老人對孩子的"鐘愛"，並不是簡單的 love，譯文二用 I was the apple of her eye，與原意相符。

7）**伺候**——這個詞在不同的語境里意思不盡相同，例如：伺候病人 — to attend a patient，"伺候人的工作我不喜歡。"—I don't want to do the job of waiting on people. 這里的"伺候"，不是"照顧"，而是"討好人，讓人高興"的意思，所以用 please。

》 例文三

兩人世界

在中國，晚婚晚育的人越來越多了，不要孩子的年輕夫婦也越來越多了。這些人大多數是**知識分子**，而且主要是在北京、廣州和上海這樣的大城市。1979 年到 1989 年是中國開始改革開放的頭十年，據調查，在這十年間，上海有 16 萬對新婚夫婦一直沒要孩子，占上海新婚夫婦總數的 14%。現在就更多了。

他們這樣做是有多種原因的：有的是出於家庭經濟方面的考慮；有的是因為忙於事業；還有的跟**愛情因素**有關係。

北京有一位護士，結婚九年了一直不要孩子，她說："我們倆特愛旅遊，特愛看電影，有時候半夜三更才回家。要是有了孩子，**就有了拖累，時間就全搭給他了**。"

還有些人認為**生孩子、養孩子會影響他們的事業**，他們沒有辦法又要孩子，又要事業。為了事業，他們寧願放棄**天倫之樂**。有些年輕人婚後仍然繼續進修，哪有時間養孩子？他們這樣做倒不完全是為了得學位、拿文憑，而是要**提高生活質量**。

不要孩子的夫婦 60% 都讀過大學，這說明人的**受教育程度起了決定作用**。

譯文一

A World of Two

In China, more and more people prefer late marriage and late childbirth and even a no-child family. This is especially true with *intellectuals* and in big cities like Beijing, Shanghai and Guangzhou.

According to a survey, from 1979 to 1989, when China first opened its door to the outside world, in shanghai 160 thousand couples, which accounted for 14% of the couples married in that period, did not have children. And the number has been increasing.

There are various reasons for their choice, *some are economic and some emotional.* And many people are too busy with their work or study to have children.

A nurse in Beijing, having been married for nine years, *hasn't got a child.* She said, "My husband and I are avid travelers and cinema-goers. And we often stay out late. If we had a child, we would be confined to home all the time."

Some think that a child may take up too much time and hold up progress in their career. To pursue success, they have to give up the happiness of having a child. Some young couples further their own education even after they get married. They are not only interested in getting diplomas or degrees, but *to improve their standard of living.*

60% of the Dinky families are college graduates, which shows that one's educational background plays a decisive role.

譯文二

Dinks in China

In China, a growing number of people *choose* late marriage and *delayed* childbirth, or no-child family. This is the case with most of *the educated young people* in big cities like Beijing, Shanghai and Guangzhou.

A survey shows that in Shanghai 160,000 or 14% of couples who married in the ten years from 1979 to 1989 when China first opened up did not have any children. And this number has been increasing since.

Economic factors and husband-and-wife relationship played a part in their choice. And many of them were too busy building a career to afford any children.

A nurse in Beijing has remained childless since she got married nine years ago.

She said, "My husband and I travel a great deal and we like going to the cinema. We often stay out late. A child would *keep us home all the time*."

Some of the dinks say that kids would *claim too much of the time which they need to pursue a career.* So they have to live a life deprived of *the joy that a child might bring to the family.* Others have opted for continued education, not just for diplomas or degrees, but mainly to improve the quality of their life.

60% of dinks are college graduates, which shows that one's educational background *plays a decisive role in family planning.*

【分析】這是一篇報刊評論文,簡略報道了一個時期中國的婚姻狀況。文中有些用詞在英譯時必須先解釋清楚,否則就會給英語讀者的理解帶來一定的困難。具體分析如下:

1) **兩人世界**——這是漢語中比較時髦的詞,譯文一直譯成了 A World of Two,英語讀者會迷惑不解,譯文二譯為 Dinks in China,體現了原意:"不要孩子的家庭"。

2) **知識分子**——在漢語中這是一個有高度概括性的詞,涉及的範圍很廣,包括所有受過教育的人,其中有專家學者等高級"知識分子",大學畢業具有學士、碩士學位的中級"知識分子"和高中畢業等初級"知識分子"。但是這個詞並不等於譯文一中所用的 intellectuals。Intellectuals 一詞主要指那些善於思考的學者(highly educated people whose interests are studying and other activities that involve careful thinking and mental effort)。本文中的"知識分子"其實僅指那些受過高等教育的人。所以譯文二譯成 *the educated young people* 是正確的。

3) **愛情因素**——這是非常含糊的表達方式,如果譯成 factors of love 或 emotional factors,譯文讀者會弄不清其中的意思,因此,我們必須先解釋,後翻譯。其實"愛情因素"指的就是"夫妻關係":husband-and-wife relationship。

4) **拖累**——這個詞脫離了語境,便失去了依托,可以指很多給人以拖累的事情,如:家務拖累:burdened with household chores,家庭拖累:having a family to support。那麼,這裏的拖累是什麼呢? 從上下文來看,這個"拖累"指的是"有了孩子,他們就不能出去旅遊了",所以要釋譯為:A child would keep us home all the time。

5) **生孩子、養孩子會影響他們的事業**——"有了孩子,就沒了事業",現在很多年輕人都持這個觀點。但是孩子是如何影響事業的? 漢語原文沒有講,但英譯文必須解釋清楚:Kids would claim too much of the time which they need to pursue a career,"養孩子占用了他們本來用來學習、進修、創事業的時間",而不是像譯文一所譯：hold up progress in their career，"妨礙了他們在事業上的進步"。

6）**天倫之樂**——這個詞泛指家庭帶來的快樂，但這裡不能譯為 family love and happiness，或 happiness of a family living together，必須明確解釋為"孩子給父母帶來的快樂"：the joy that a child might bring to the family。

7）**提高生活質量**——這個提法非常籠統，既可以指"提高生活水平"，也可以指"生活豐富多彩"，還可以指"生活舒適自在"，所以這裡也只好籠統對之：to improve the quality of their life。譯文一的譯法 to improve their standard of living 過於具體。

8）**受教育程度起了決定作用**——在哪方面起了決定作用？漢語中沒說，但英語裡必須有：One's educational background plays a decisive role *in family planning*。

》 例文四

中國孩子太辛苦

郭瑩

原文：

中國孩子實在是**太辛苦了**，一個十歲的孩子一天的典型日程表是這樣的：清晨 6 點 30 分爬起來匆匆趕往學校上**早自習**，下午 5 點放學後再跑到**英語補習班**去進修，晚上要忙到午夜前一刻，才筋疲力盡地做完**老師及家長布置的雙重作業**。日復一日，年復一年，家長的目標是使孩子長大了爭當**"哈佛女孩"、"牛津男孩"**。

有一個二十歲的青年，**一瞧見鋼琴就厭惡**。他曾向我訴說其童年是多麼的不快樂。每天有做不完的家庭作業，還得學鋼琴、繪畫和補習英語，儘管他根本沒有音樂天賦，每天在媽媽的眼皮底下按那些枯燥的琴鍵如同受刑。媽媽還動不動就念叨：你只要抓緊時間學習，媽媽就高興。**這簡直是在折磨孩子的童年。**

——《讀者》，2003

譯文一

Chinese Children Are Overworked

Most Chinese children are really *having a hard time with their study.* Take a typical daily schedule of a ten-year-old. Having got up at 6:30 a.m., he must dash to school to *prepare his lessons* for the day and after school at 5 p.m., he has to go to an extracurricular class, usually English *to get special training.* Having come home, he must finish his endless *homework assigned by both his teachers and parents.* Usually he cannot go to bed until midnight. He has to follow this schedule day in and day out the whole year round, just because his parents want him to go to a renowned university, such as Harvard and Oxford.

A twenty-year-old young man told me he always felt sick at the sight of a piano, because he was forced to have piano lessons after a day's work at school when he was little. In addition, he had to attend drawing and English classes at the weekends. He said he was not gifted in music, so it was torture for him sitting at the piano and hearing his mother babbling that she was pleased as long as he worked hard. What a torment it was for a little kid!

譯文二

How Exhausted They Are

Most of Chinese children are **over-loaded with schoolwork.** This is a typical day of a ten-year-old kid: Up at 6:30 a. m. , so the child would be able to make the **morning private study sessions** at school; by 5 p. m. , when **school closes,** the kid dashes to **extracurricular classes, usually those teaching English.** Evenings at home mean endless **homework assigned by the parents in addition to that by the teachers.** That will keep the kid up until midnight. That's the schedule the poor child has to follow year in and year out, just to be able **to make the grade** of a "Harvard girl" or "Oxford boy" as his or her parents hope.

A twenty-year-old young man told me the sight of a piano made him sick. The instrument, he said, would **bring back to his mind his school days when he had to take piano lessons against his will**, in addition to painting and English classes he had to attend on weekends, even though he had no talent for music. That's why playing on the keyboard was torture for him, and his mother's babbling made it even worse although she kept saying how pleased she would be to see him work hard at these things. **You can imagine how painful the memory of his childhood can be.**

【分析】這也是一篇報刊評論文章,簡略報道了長期以來中國小學生的課業負擔過重的現象及原因。其中有很多表達方式極具中國特色,不加解釋的直譯是不能把原意傳達過去的。具體分析如下:

1) **太辛苦**——"辛苦"一詞在不同的語境中有很多不同的用法和功能,但是,其基本含義是 working hard。然而在翻譯中不能一律照此辦理。例如:

"這是件**辛苦的**工作。"——It's **hard** work.

"同志們**辛苦了**！"——**How are you**, comrades！

"您就再**辛苦一趟**吧。"——I'm afraid you have to **take the trouble to go there** again.

"他把多年**辛苦搜集**的古董捐給了國家博物館。" ——He donated all the antiques he **had taken great pains to collect** over the years to the National Museum.

這里的"辛苦"明顯是指課業太重：over-loaded with schoolwork，譯文一的譯法 having a hard time with their study 不是漢語原文本意，而是"學習上很吃力"的意思。

2）**早自習**——譯文一譯成 prepare his lessons for the day，這樣譯給人的感覺像是在說教師備課或大學生的早自習。其實小學生是不應該有早自習的，這里只能籠統地翻作 morning private study sessions。

3）**英語補習班**——這也是中國特有的事物，對於大多數孩子說來，英語是最難學的科目，因此，多數學生都要參加補習班：extracurricular classes, usually those teaching English，而不是像譯文一所譯：to get special training，這倒成了進修班或提高班了。

4）**老師及家長布置的雙重作業。**——家長給孩子布置額外的作業也是中國特有的事物，必須解釋清楚，homework assigned by the parents **in addition to** that by the teachers.

5）**爭當"哈佛女孩"、"牛津男孩"**——這句話指的是要孩子努力學習，將來達到上名牌大學的標準：**to make the grade** of a "Harvard girl" or "Oxford boy" as his or her parents hope.

6）**一瞧見鋼琴就厭惡**——為什麼"一瞧見鋼琴就厭惡"呢？原文沒說清楚，譯文必須解釋：The instrument, he said, would **bring back to his mind his school days when he had to take piano lessons against his will**，鋼琴總讓他想起小的時候被迫學琴的經歷。

7）**這簡直是在折磨孩子的童年。**——這是病句，只能"折磨人"，不能"折磨童年"。最後一句話應該帶有總結性：You can imagine how painful the memory of his childhood can be.

例文五

那晚睡不著

吳祖光

原文：

時常和母親要錢，又說不出個正經的用處，是一件很**不舒服的**事情。因此在一天清早,所有的人在睡覺,只有我一個人很早起床時,看見桌上放著一疊銅子,便不免心喜,**拿了**一小部分放在口袋里上學去了。

當時曾經想到,這就是"偷東西"嗎? **略微有些不安**,但**想不到這些了**,並且始終沒有人發覺,於是這便成了我**日常的習慣**。

胃口越吃越大之時,終有一天**落網了**。有一回我一狠之下把桌上的一打疊銅子全部裝進衣袋,偏偏母親馬上就來拿錢,馬上注意到了我,結果從我的衣袋里破獲了全部的贓物。

母親**半晌無語**,看了我許久,說:你拿這些錢做什麼? 我低了頭說"我想買乒乓球,還有網子、拍子……"

母親說:"這是偷錢,做賊,懂嗎?"又過了一會兒說,"到學校里去,**回來再跟你說**。"

晚上我很早就睡了,主要的原因是怕父親回來。其實我哪里睡得著呢。

我聽見父親回來後問:"他睡著了嗎?"母親說:"睡著了。"父親說:"把這個放在這兒吧。"我**面朝里裝睡**,感覺到母親把一樣東西輕輕擺在我枕頭旁邊。

第二天清晨醒來時,我一把抱住了枕邊的盒子。打開盒子,看到里面是兩個球拍,一面網子,半打乒乓球。

父親、母親、祖母以後都沒有再提過這椿事,而我也沒有再偷錢。

——《上海家庭報》,2006-11-24

譯文一

A Sleepless Night

When I was a little boy, it was ***very embarrassing*** to ask money from my parents without a proper reason. In an early morning, while all others were still sleeping, I got up. I felt very pleased to see a pile of coppers on the table and ***put some in my pocket.***

Although I was a little bit guilty wondering whether it was stealing, I was quite happy not to be discovered. And since then it ***became a habit of taking some pocket money that way.***

Having got more and more greedy, one day I took all the money from the table and put it in my pocket. At that time my mom was just coming to get the money, I was caught red-handed. She uncovered all the spoils from my pocket.

Speechless, she looked at me for quite a while. Then she asked, "What do you want the money for?" "To buy ping-pong paddles, balls and a net…" I answered.

"This is a theft, you know?" she said. "Go to school now. ***Wait until you come*** *back.*"

That night I went to bed very early mainly for fear of seeing my father. How could I fall asleep at that time?

I heard my daddy come back and ask my mom, "Is he asleep now?"

"Yes," she said.

"Put this here."

I pretended to be asleep and felt mom put something gently beside my pillow.

The next morning when I woke up, I saw a box and opened it immediately. There were two ping-pong paddles, a net and half a dozen balls in it.

Neither my daddy, my mom nor my grandmother ever mentioned this later and *I've never stolen money again* since then.

譯文二

I Couldn't Sleep That Night

I found it very *unpleasant* to ask my mother for money, as I often did, and unable to tell her what I needed it for. One morning, when I got up and all the others were still sleeping, I was thrilled to find a pile of coppers on the table. I *helped myself to* some of them and went to school.

This gave me a bit of qualms, as I wondered if it was steeling. But *when my doubts were gone*, and I was never caught, *I became bold.*

My appetite kept growing until I was *nabbed* doing it. One day just as I had put all the coins from the table in my pocket, my mother came for them and saw what I was doing. I had to surrender to her all the spoils. I had been caught red-handed.

My mother was stunned. She stared at me for quite a while before she asked, "What do you want so much money for?" "To buy ping-pong paddles, balls and a net..." I answered, bending my head in shame.

"This is stealing. You're a thief, *you know*?" adding after a long silence, "Go to school now. We'll settle this when you come back."

I went to bed early that night mainly to avoid seeing my father. But how could I sleep?

When my father returned, I heard him asking my mother, "Is he sleeping?"

"Yes," she said.

"Leave this here."

With my back turned away from them, ***I was pretending to*** be ***sleeping*** when I felt my mother was putting something gently next to my pillow.

The next morning when I woke up, I grabbed what my mother had left in my bed. It was a box. I opened it. It had two ping-pong paddles, half a dozen balls and a net in it.

My father, my mother and my grandmother never talked about the incident again in all the years after it, and that was the last time ***I pinched money.***

【分析】原文作者吳祖光，現代劇作家。這是他的一篇小品散文，生動地描繪了大多數人孩童時代都有過的經歷，語言樸素自然，但仍具有典型的漢語特點，在英譯選詞時需作一些解釋。詳細分析如下：

1) **不舒服的事**——"不舒服"的用法太廣了，脫離了上下文就很難確定詞義，例如：

"你哪兒**不舒服**?"——What's ***wrong with*** you?

"我今天**不舒服**。"——I'm ***out of sorts*** today.

"我坐在這兒**不舒服**。"——I'm ***not comfortable*** sitting here.

這里的"不舒服"是"令人不快"的意思，所以要用 unpleasant 對之。譯文一中所用的 embarrassing 一詞是"使人尷尬"的意思，與原文中的"不舒服"意思相差甚遠。

2) **拿了(錢)**——這里的"拿錢"不是像譯文一所譯的那樣，隨隨便便地 put some coins in my pocket，而是 to take some money without permission，所以要用 I helped myself to some of them。

3) **略微有些不安**——這里的"不安"是指 a feeling of doubt or worry about whether what you have done is right，所以要用 qualm 一詞。譯文一中用了 guilty，意思是 feeling ashamed because you have done something you know is wrong，顯然是不對的。

4) **想不到這些了**——這句話的意思是"不去想這麼多了"，所以譯成 when my doubts were gone，意思是"沒有了疑慮，不再擔心"。

5) **成了我日常的習慣**——這里的"習慣"與 habit 沒關係，意思只是"膽子越來越大"，因此，譯成 I became bold 和 My appetite kept growing。譯文一中的 it became a habit of taking some pocket money that way，演繹的成分太多。

6) **落網**——這里是諧謔用法，必須用個非正式的詞對之，譯文二中的 nab 比較合適。

7) **母親半晌無語**——這里的"半晌無語"不僅是不說話，里邊暗含著"母親被驚呆了,一句話也說不出來"的意思,所以譯文一中只用 speechless,意思不到位,譯文二譯成 My mother was stunned,解釋得很合適。

8) **我面朝里裝睡**——這句話說明作者的床是靠牆的,這里不必過多解釋,譯成 With my back turned away from them 即可。

9) **我也沒有再偷錢**——這里的"偷錢",還是指作者未經允許拿錢一事,譯文一所譯 have stolen money 過於正式,譯成非正式的 pinch 在本文的上下文中較為合適。

思考題

1. 在什麼情況下必須對漢語原文中的詞或句子先進行解釋,然後再翻譯?
2. 為什麼在篇章翻譯中要講求釋義性翻譯法?

第十七章　譯文的綜合潤色和檢審

　　篇章翻譯始於通讀原文，終於審讀譯文。譯文的終稿審讀包括兩個方面：宏觀審閱和微觀潤色。宏觀審閱是檢查譯文是否通順流暢，行文是否能給人以美感，篇章的主旨、風格以及文體與原文有無大的出入。微觀潤色是檢查用詞是否準確貼切、句子是否精練簡約。正像陸機在《文賦》（並序）中所說的，"要詞達而理舉，故無取乎冗長"。微觀潤色是包含在宏觀審閱過程中的，只有統觀全局，才能檢查局部；只有在閱讀全篇的語流中，才能體現譯者的語感。許多拙詞、拗句只有在全局性審讀中，使譯者產生語感障礙，才能發現。潤色詞語的標準是準確、精練、雋美，也就是嚴復的信達雅原則：用詞準確以求"信"，組句精練以求"達"，謀篇雋美以求"雅"。那些詞不切意，文不順理，句不悅美的粗糙、蕪雜的文字都要在譯文終稿審讀中剔除，以使譯文達到讀來自然流暢、簡練悅耳的美學效果。

　　下面對實例進行具體分析。

≫ 例文一

圖書館

原文：

　　四十幾年前，我**初到臺灣**，一無所有，生活都有困難，買書更是奢望。後來，通過念經、法會，自己有了一些錢，就全數拿來買書。

　　同學們看到我將錢花在買書上，便問我："你的錢不拿來買穿的、吃的，干嗎老是買書呢？"

　　我說："我將來要辦圖書館！"

　　他們聽我這麼說，哈哈大笑："**你真是做夢**，還想辦圖書館？"

　　我沒理會他們的嘲諷，依舊一有錢，就拿來買書。就這樣買了幾十年，從中文書籍,到日文、英文、俄文、西班牙文、法文書籍,從佛教書籍,到哲學、文學、歷史、傳記書籍。到現在,不但自己閱讀了許多書,而且**創建了二十六個圖書館。**

王安石說:"貧者因書而富,富者因書而貴。"一個學校的生命,就在圖書館;一個人的生命就在閱讀。所以我寧願將自己的收入用來買書,以供大眾暢遊於圖書法海中,讓每個人都能因書而富貴,透過書去看看世界,讀讀古今,在書中,振翅高飛。

——星雲大師:《禪師的米粒》

譯文一

My Libraries

When I first came to Taiwan over forty years ago, I was such a poor **Buddhist disciple** that I could not even make ends meet and to buy books was really a luxury for me. Later on I began to make some money by giving Buddhist services, such as chanting scriptures. I spent almost all the money buying books.

Seeing this, my fellow disciples asked me, "Why do you spend all your money on books instead of buying daily necessities?"

"I will establish a library." I said.

Hearing this, they all laughed and said, "Establish a library? What a dream you have!"

Ignoring their ridicules, I kept buying books as soon as I had money. I persevered for tens of years buying books of various languages ranging from Chinese to Japanese, English, Russian, Spanish and French. The subjects of the books covered not only Buddhism, but also philosophy, literature, history and biography. In those years I read a lot of books and at last I have had 26 libraries established.

The Chinese scholar Wang Anshi (1021 – 1086) said, "***By reading the poor can get well-off and the well-off noble.*** *The library is the soul of a school and reading is the lifeblood for a person.* That is why I have devoted all my income to books. I wish everybody can have an access to books, become rich and noble and learn about history, the present and the magnificent world through reading.

譯文二

My Libraries

When I first came to Taiwan over forty years ago, I was a poor **Buddhist monk** who could not make ends meet, to say nothing of buying books. Later when I could make some money by giving Buddhist services, such as chanting scriptures, **presiding over religious assemblies**, I spent almost all of it on books.

My friends wondered why I was spending so much on books as to deny myself of the basic needs of my life, I said, "**I'm trying to build a library.**"

They all laughed and called me crazy.

I didn't care what they called me; I kept buying books whenever I had the money for them. This went on for several decades. The books I bought included those in foreign languages: Japanese, English, Russian, Spanish and French, on subjects ranging from Buddhism, philosophy, literature, history and biography. I didn't buy these books just for **my own reading pleasure**; I had twenty-six libraries **stocked with them**.

The Song scholar Wang Anshi(1021 – 1086) said, "**Books bring the poor wealth and the rich honor.**" As no school is complete without a library, so meaningless is life without books. I spend every penny I earn on books because I believe books should be made accessible to all, so **we will become informed of the world now and then in our quest for wealth and fame.**

【分析】這是我國臺灣省著名的佛教法師星雲大師所著的散文節選,主旨是人生要以學為本。行文簡練自然,其中富含中文語言特色,譯成英文要費一番躊躇。

1) **我初到臺灣,一無所有**——星雲大師以什麼身分到了臺灣?原文沒有,譯文必須有:他初到臺灣,必然不是大師,只能是個和尚。譯文一所譯的 Buddhist disciple 是不對的,因為 disciple 是指某人的弟子。譯文二用的 Buddhist monk 意思準確。

2) **同學們看到我將錢花在買書上,便問我……**——這里的"同學"所指不明,可能是與大師一起修煉的師兄弟,也可能是一般夥伴。譯文一中的 my fellow disciples 是誤譯,譯文二權且譯作 my friends 很合適。譯文一用直接引語,按照原文譯成對話,不妥,因為大師的同學嘲笑他的話並不重要,直接引用會使行文顯得拖沓。譯文二改譯為間接引語,只保留了一個重要句子:"I'm trying to build a library",既突出了重點,又使敘述簡練。

3) **你真是做夢**——原文里的這句話帶有貶義,是"痴人說夢""異想天開"的意思,而譯文一所譯的 What a dream you have! 帶有很大程度的褒義,可以說是一句讚揚的話,意為"有理想""願望好"。這句話最好譯成 They all laughed and called me crazy。

4) **我沒理會他們的嘲諷**——這句話要與上一句 called me crazy 保持連貫,所以譯成 I didn't care what they called me。而譯文一所譯的 Ignoring their ridicules 略顯生硬,因為 ignore 一詞有"故意不理睬"的意思,而此處的"沒理會"是"不在意"的意思。

5) **創建了二十六個圖書館。**——這里的"創建"肯定不包括土木工程,所以 to build, to establish 都不合適,星雲大師"創建"圖書館,是購買足夠的書以充館藏,所以譯成 I had twenty-six libraries stocked with them.

6) **貧者因書而富,富者因書而貴。**——這是王安石的一句名言,譯文一所譯: By reading the poor can get well-off and the well-off noble 不太貼切。reading 不光指讀書,它包含的內容很廣,也可以是讀報、看雜志等。well-off 的意思是 having sufficient money for comfortable living,並不是一定十分"富有",不如 rich 簡短、達意。noble 特指"品格高尚"。譯文二所譯:Books bring the poor wealth and the rich honor. 簡約精當,語體更適於名人名言。honor 一詞概括了 great respect and admiration,譯得到位。

7) **一個學校的生命就在圖書館;一個人的生命就在閱讀。**——這句話是典型的中國式表達,富於詩意。譯文一基本是照原句直譯 The library is the soul of a school and reading is the lifeblood for a person,不太符合英語的表達習慣,而且帶有很強的學生腔,用 and 連接兩句話也顯囉唆。譯文二就貼切多了:As no school is complete without a library, so meaningless is life without books. Life is meaningless without books 是主句,也是全篇主旨,而 As no school is complete without a library 是從句,起著比較、襯托的作用。

8) **以供大眾暢遊於圖書法海中,讓每個人都能因書而富貴,透過書去看看世界,讀讀古今,在書中,振翅高飛。**——這又是典型的富於詩意的漢語表達法。尤其是"暢遊於圖書法海中""在書中,振翅高飛",更有漢語特點,英譯文要減少這些特點,使之符合英語習慣,所以譯文二所譯更為簡練、達意:We will become informed of the world now and then in our quest for wealth and fame.

≫ 例文二

可憐的花

陳輯

原文：

我朋友**愛養花,什麼花都栽得很好。**

每到花開季節,滿園子花香宜人,蝶飛蜂繞,很讓人羨慕。於是,我和一幫朋友時常去他家賞花。朋友是個大方人,碰上**愛花人**,必以鮮花相贈,所以,有許多人慕名而來。

一天,我去他家時,碰上張三也在那里,正纏著我朋友不放,討要一盆開得正艷的牡丹。奇怪的是,平素大方的朋友**一反常態**,說啥也不想給。

好在都是熟人,**實在卻不過情面**。張三懇求再三,硬是把花搬走了。我朋友頓腳嘆息說:"不信你等著看吧,**這棵花算是死定了。**"

果然,沒過多久,張三搬走的牡丹就死了。朋友**搖頭惋惜**:"果然不出所料啊!"我問為什麼。

朋友說:"難道你看不出,張三這人是勢利眼嗎?別人發達時,他趨之若鶩;別人倒霉時,他避之不及。"

我問:"這跟養花又有什麼關係?"

朋友正色道:"**用這份性情來養花,必然是花艷時百般呵護,花謝時棄之不顧。你想想看,世上又有哪一朵花可以永開不敗的呢?**"

——《益壽文摘》,2008(33)

譯文一

A Pitiful Peony

I have a friend who is ***good at growing flowers*** and whatever flower grows well in his hands.

His garden is always an admirable sight with beautiful flowers and sweet fragrance in the spring which attract bees and butterflies here. Therefore quite a lot of his friends often go there to feast their eyes on the flowers. And my friend is a generous person and often gives flowers to ***those who ask for them.*** So a lot of visitors come to his garden to look at or ***demand flowers.***

One day I went to his place and happened to see Zhang San there, who was pestering my friend for a peony which was in full bloom. Surprisingly enough, my friend, **unlike his usual behavior**, refused Zhang San's demand. Finally, not wanting to hurt his feelings, my friend reluctantly let Zhang San take the peony away. Then he stamped his feet and sighed: "**The peony is bound to die. You'll see.**"

Soon after, the flower did die. My friend **shook his head with sadness** and said: "So you see, just as I expected." I asked about the reason.

My friend answered: "Can't you see Zhang San is a real snob? **He flatters successful people and avoids those who have bad luck.**"

"What does that have anything to do with flowers?" I asked.

He answered in a grave tone: "**A snob must treat flowers with the same attitude as to people. He would cherish the blooming flowers most dearly and cast aside the withering ones. Is it possible for any flower to remain fresh all the time in this world?**"

譯文二

In Wrong Hands

I have a friend who is a **horticultural expert.** He has a garden, a lovely place which, with its meticulously cared-for flowers filling the air their fragrance, attracts bees, butterflies and admirers, me and my friends included. My friend is a generous person who enjoys giving his flowers to **flower-fanciers** who come to his garden. That explains why visitors come the garden **in droves**.

One day when I was in his place, I met Zhang San. He was pestering my friend with his request for one of the peonies in full bloom as a gift for him. To my surprise, my friend refused, and adamantly, **which was not like him**. But Zhang insisted. Afraid that he might **hurt the pride of his friend**, my friend conceded to his request, and Zhang left with what he wanted.

After Zhang left, my friend said with much pain in his voice, "**My poor peony**! It's doomed.**"

Sure enough, the flower soon died. When my friend learned of that **he said sadly**, "I knew this would happen." He explained, "Don't you see Zhang San is a snob? He **flatters the rich and despises the poor.**"

"What does that have to do with flowers?" I asked.

"**Snobs treat flowers,**" he answered philosophically, "**the way they treat people. They will take the best care they can of flowers when they are at their best**

and will trash them when they wither，***but is it possible for flowers to stay in bloom all the time***？"

　　【分析】這是一篇富於哲理的小品文,諷刺了歷史上和現實中都存在的趨炎附勢的勢利眼。本文文筆流暢、情趣盎然,但其中有多處是典型的中式表達法,英譯時要注意。

　　1)**可憐的花**——這是本文的題目,譯文一直譯為 A Pitiful Peony,可以說是誤譯,沒有忠實原文,因為用 pitiful 來修飾花草,是指花草長得很弱,瀕於死亡。譯文二譯成 In Wrong Hands 是根據全篇的中心思想,給英譯文取的一個題目,意思是"花草到了不同人的手裡,命運也就不同了。"

　　2)**愛養花,什麼花都栽得很好**——譯文一譯成 good at growing flowers,顯得囉嗦,意思也不充分,譯文二直接譯為英語中現成的詞:horticultural expert,既表達了原文意思,又符合英語語言習慣,可以說是言簡意賅。

　　3)**愛花人**——譯文一所譯的 those who ask for them 和 demand flowers,也是放著現有詞匯不用,而硬譯原文,既生硬,又囉唆。譯文二用了現成的詞 flower-fanciers,既自然,又貼切。

　　4)**一反常態**——譯文一的譯法 unlike his usual behavior 是硬譯,因為 behavior 一詞是比較籠統、正式的詞,意為 the way a person behaves in a particular situation,在這裡顯然不合適。

　　5)**實在卻不過情面**——"情面"是中國人在交往中比較重視的事情,意思比較寬泛,可以理解為"面子"、"自尊"或某種場合中的"一個人的心情"。在本文中應是"自尊",所以譯文二的譯法正確:(not to) hurt the pride of his friend,譯文一譯成 not wanting to hurt his feelings,是"不傷感情",意思與原文不符。

　　6)**這棵花算是死定了**——譯文一的譯法 The peony is bound to die,不如譯文二生動、自然:My poor peony! It's doomed.

　　7)**搖頭惋惜**——譯文一的直譯 shook his head with sadness 明顯有誤,因為在英語國家,人們"搖頭"不一定表示"惋惜",譯成 he said sadly 就已經到位了。

　　8)**朋友正色道:"用這份性情來養花,必然是花艷時百般呵護,花謝時棄之不顧。你想想看,世上又有哪一朵花可以永開不敗的呢?"**——這句話是本文所要闡明的要旨,是給那些"勢利眼"所下的結論,要有"畫龍點睛"的效果,從這個角度考慮,譯文二所譯甚佳:"Snobs treat flowers," he answered philosophically, "the way they treat people. They will take the best care they can of flowers when they are at their best and will trash them when they wither, but is it possible for flowers to stay in bloom all the time?"尤其是 he answered philosophically 一句,起到了傳達原文雖未明言,但有暗指的意思。

例文三

華羅庚的求學之路

原文：

華羅庚在十七歲時便身患傷寒，貧病中臥床半年致使左腿殘廢。也就在此後的幾年中，他全靠自學讀完了從高中到大學的八年課程，**後來他學業成就卓著，受聘到清華大學任教，**但當時表上填的仍是初中畢業生。

1936 年，華羅庚初到劍橋大學留學，著名數學家哈代正在美國旅行，此前他曾看過推薦華羅庚的信和華羅庚的論文，就給另一位數學家海爾布倫留了一張便條："華來時，請轉告他，他可以用兩年的時間獲得博士學位。"通常若要在劍橋大學獲得博士學位，至少要三四年甚至更長的時間。海爾布倫問華羅庚："你打算攻讀哪一門課程？我們給你提供幫助。"華羅庚回答說："謝謝你的好意。我只有兩年的研究時間，自然要多學點東西，多寫些**有意思的文章**。念博士不免有些**繁文縟節**，太浪費時間了。我不想念博士學位，我只要求做一個訪問學者。我來劍橋大學是為了求學問，不是為了學位。"

海爾布倫聞言，不覺大感意外："東方來的人，不稀罕劍橋大學的博士學位者，你還是第一個。我們歡迎你這樣的訪問學者。"

就在那裡的一年當中，華羅庚完成了十一篇論文。而這些論文，**每一篇都可得到一個博士學位。**

1979 年 11 月，華羅庚來到法國南錫大學，參加為授予他榮譽博士學位而舉行的隆重儀式。**從此他才有了比初中畢業更高的學銜，這年，他已經 68 歲了。**

——梁東元：《傾聽大師們的聲音》

譯文一

Hua Luogeng's Pursuit of Education

Hua Luogeng, Chinese renowned mathematician, began his education the hardest way. When he was 17 years old, he suffered from typhoid. He was confined to bed for half a year. Being very poor and not having got proper treatment for his disease, he became crippled. Not having flinched in the face of tremendous difficulties, he completed the courses from senior high to college by teaching himself. *Later on he became a teacher in Qinghua University with only a secondary-school diploma.*

In 1936, when Hua Luogeng came to Cambridge University, Hardy, the famous Cambridge mathematician was traveling in America. Before he left England he had received a letter of recommendation for Hua and his research papers. He left a message to Heilbronn, his colleague, which said, "When Hua comes, please tell him he can get a doctor's degree here in two years." The usual time to get a doctor's degree in Cambridge was three or four years or even longer. Then when Heilbronn saw Hua, he asked him, "What subject do you want to study? We'll help you." Hearing this, Hua said, "I appreciate your kindness, but I'll have only two years of research here. I want to study as much as possible and **write meaningful papers.** To get a doctor's degree, I would have to get through much **red tape**, which would take me a lot of time. So I just want to be a visiting scholar instead of getting a doctor's degree, for I came here to seek knowledge, not a degree."

Very astonished, Heilbronn said, "You are the first Asian I've ever seen who is not interested in getting a doctor's degree in Cambridge. And we are glad to have a visiting scholar like you."

In just one year there, Hua Luogeng wrote 11 research papers, and each one of them was **good enough** for him to have got a doctor's degree.

In November 1979, Hua Luogeng went to attend the ceremony of receiving his honorary doctor's degree conferred by Nancy University in France. Only by then, at the age of 68, he got a degree higher than a secondary-school diploma.

譯文二

The Education of Hua Luogeng

Hua Luogeng, **the renowned Chinese mathematician**, who grew up in poverty, was 17 years old when he was struck by typhoid, which, after confining him to bed for half a year, left him crippled in the left leg.

He won a teaching position at the prestigious Qinghua University, **not on the strength of his formal education, which ended when he finished 3rd year junior high, but on what he had achieved, all by self-teaching**, in all the academic courses from senior high school to college.

In 1936, when Hua Luogeng came to Cambridge University, Hardy, the famous mathematician, was traveling in America. Before he left England he had received a letter of recommendation for Hua along with his research papers. He left a message to

Heilbronn, his colleague, which said, "When Hua comes, please tell him he can get his doctor's degree here in two years." At Cambridge the study for a PhD degree took three or four years, or longer. When Heilbronn saw him, he asked him, "What is the subject you intend to study? We may help you." "Thank you for your kindness," Hua said, "I have only two years to do research here. I would like to study as much and produce as many ***useful papers*** as the two years allow me. I am not here to pursue a doctoral degree. That would cost me too much time ***going through all the formalities.*** I'm here just as a visiting scholar, not after a PhD. Study is the sole purpose of my being here."

Heilbronn was surprised. "You are the first Asian I've ever met who's not interested in getting a doctor's degree from Cambridge," he said. "A scholar like you is more than welcome here."

In just one year, Hua Luogeng produced eleven research papers, and each one of them was ***strong enough to earn him a doctor's degree.***

In November 1979, Hua Luogeng was awarded an honorary doctoral degree by Nancy University in France in recognition of his academic position, which was much higher than that of a holder of a junior high diploma. He was then 68.

【分析】上文摘自名人傳記型的報告文學,講述了數學大師華羅庚一生中最能體現其大師風範的片段。文章開頭沒有給華羅庚做介紹,因為幾十年來華羅庚的名字在中國家喻戶曉,但在英譯文中必須加以說明: the renowned Chinese mathematician。

　　1) **後來他學業成就卓著,受聘到清華大學任教**——一個初中畢業生能夠受聘到清華大學任教,在西方國家是不可思議的事,因此在譯文中必須加以說明: He won a teaching position at the prestigious Qinghua University, ***not on the strength of his formal education, which ended when he finished*** 3rd ***year junior high, but on what he had achieved, all by self-teaching***…

　　2) **有意思的文章**——這句話的意思十分模糊,譯文一翻譯為 meaningful papers,欠妥,這會讓人理解為別人寫的文章都是 meaningless。譯文二譯成 useful papers,很合適,說明華羅庚打算寫一些有實際效益的文章,以解決實際問題。

　　3) **繁文縟節**——這個詞在這裡並不是指政府部門煩瑣的公事程序,所以譯文一譯成 red tape,就是誤譯。"繁文縟節"這裡指的是要讀學位,就必須通過必要的但很麻煩的手續,如寫論文開題報告、找導師指導論文、答辯等。因此 going through all the formalities 是正確的譯法。

4）**每一篇都可得到一個博士學位**——為什麼十一篇論文"每一篇都可得到一個博士學位"？原文沒說明，譯者也無從知曉，但是，按照常識，我們可以認為華羅庚的論文一定非常 strong，意思是 firmly established，difficult to destroy。譯文一譯成 good enough 力度不夠。

5）**從此他才有了比初中畢業更高的學銜，這年，他已經 68 歲了。**——譯文一是 Only by then，***at the age of*** 68，he got a degree higher than a secondary-school diploma。譯文二是 Hua Luogeng was awarded an honorary doctoral degree by Nancy University in France in recognition of his academic position，which was much higher than that of a holder of a junior high diploma。***He was then*** 68. 在原文中，這句話的重點或精彩之處在"華羅庚 68 歲時才有了比初中畢業更高的學銜"，因此，譯文二另起一句，譯成 He was then 68，不但突出了重點，而且使整篇文章更為有力。

》 例文四

紅旗牌轎車

原文：

紅旗牌轎車是中國最早生產的豪華型高級轎車。1959 年 8 月 1 日，中國長春第一汽車製造廠製造出第一輛紅旗牌高級轎車，到 1989 年底，共生產了 1549 輛。**紅旗車車體寬大，最高時速可達 160 公里。**

紅旗轎車曾是中國國家領導人及**省部級幹部的公務用車**，1964 年，它被確定為國家級的**禮賓用車，用來接待外國來賓**。因此，在過去相當長的一段時間內，紅旗牌轎車**代表著身分和地位**。

1997 年一汽經過改進，生產出新型紅旗轎車並投入市場。這年，美國蓋洛普咨詢公司在中國消費者中進行的調查表明，在國內品牌的知名度方面，紅旗轎車排在中國銀行和青島啤酒之後，位列第三。

隨著外國汽車的不斷引進，很多新的品牌車不斷出現，雖然紅旗車仍在生產，但開紅旗車的人越來越少了。**紅旗車也少了往日的風採，也許將來有一天會退出歷史舞臺，但作為中國很長的一段歷史的見證，紅旗車會永遠留在人們的記憶中。**

譯文一

Red Flag Sedan

Red Flag Sedan was the first luxury limousine produced in China. On August 1, 1959, the Number One Automobile Manufacturing Plant in Changchun made the first Red Flag car. By the end of 1989, a total of 1549 such cars had been manufactured. The car body is wide and large, and can reach a maximum speed of 160 km/h.

Red Flag Sedan was once specially used for Chinese national leaders and high officials at the ***provincial and ministerial level.*** In 1964, it was designated to be ***the car used for ceremonial guests and visiting foreign dignitaries.*** Therefore, for many years in the past, Red Flag Sedan represented ***status and rank.***

In 1997, the Number One Automobile Manufacturing Plant improved the car and produced a new type of Red Flag Sedan which was soon introduced to the market. The American consulting company Gallup made a ***survey*** on Chinese consumers and found that in terms of their knowledge about domestic brands, Red Flag Sedan was number three, just behind the Bank of China and Qingdao Beer.

With more and more foreign cars imported in China and home-made new brands produced, the number of users of Red Flag Sedan has fallen, although the car continues to be produced. Red Flag may no longer be used in the future, but it will continue to be remembered as a very important historical witness in China.

譯文二

Red Flag

The first Red Flag ***rolled off*** the assembly line at the No. 1 Changchun Automobile Plant on August 1, 1959, marking the beginning of luxurious car making in China. By the end of 1989, 1549 Red Flags had been manufactured.

For many years, Red Flag, a wide body limousine with a top speed of 160 ***km per hour, was a status symbol*** as it was designed for use by ***government high-ranking officials on business trips***, and was added to ***the motorcades of visiting foreign VIPs in*** 1964.

In 1997 with technical innovations, Red Flag began its production for commercial purposes and soon became the third best-known brand name in China after the Bank of China and Tsingtao Beer, according to a Gallup ***poll survey.***

With the *influx* of foreign-made cars into China, and increase of new brand names in the country, *the market of Red Flag has dwindled and its halo dimmed. This decline may continue, but the brand name will remain in the collective memory of the nation.*

【分析】紅旗牌轎車曾經在 20 世紀中葉的中國歷史上發揮了重大作用,它不僅象徵著我國豪華汽車工業的發端,也見證了我國對外交往的成就,但是這一篇介紹文章寫得並不是很精彩,因此在譯文中需要潤色的地方較多。譯文一基本上是直譯,離信達雅的標準還有很大的差距,須作必要的調整。詳細分析如下:

1) **紅旗車車體寬大,最高時速可達 160 公里**——這句話在原文中單獨為一句話,但從內容上講,所在位置與上下文缺少連貫,不應成為主句,因此在譯文中將其作為同位語處理:For many years, Red Flag, *a wide body limousine with a top speed of* 160 *km per hour*, was a status symbol...

2) **省部級幹部**——譯文一直譯為 high officials at the provincial and ministerial level。其實沒有必要這樣譯,因為要外國讀者了解省部級幹部到底有多高,光這一句話還不夠,再費些筆墨,也未必能傳達出原文要說的意思。原文其實想說的就是"級別很高的官員",所以,譯文二譯成 government high-ranking officials 比較合適。

3) **公務用車**——譯文一沒有點明,不妥,譯文二譯成 on business trips 甚為妥當。

4) **禮賓用車,用來接待外國來賓**——譯文一譯成 used for ceremonial guests and visiting foreign dignitaries,意思過於籠統,譯文二譯得清楚:was added to the motorcades of visiting foreign VIPs。motorcade 是禮賓車隊,有很強的象徵意義。

5) **代表著身分和地位**——這層意思在英語中有現成的表達法:status symbol,譯文一的翻譯:represented status and rank 屬於畫蛇添足。

6) **紅旗車也少了往日的風采,也許將來有一天會退出歷史舞臺,但作為中國很長的一段歷史的見證,紅旗車會永遠留在人們的記憶中。**——這是本文的最後一句話,應該譯得有分量,但是,譯文一譯得卻很平淡:Red Flag may no longer be used in the future, but it will continue to be remembered as a very important historical witness in China。譯文二改譯為 the market of Red Flag has *dwindled* and its *halo dimmed.* This decline may continue, but the brand name will remain in the *collective memory* of the nation,突出了"雅"的效果, 其中 dwindled、halo dimmed、collective memory 是英語中現成的常用詞匯,不但達意,而且自然。尤其是 halo 一詞選得好,其意思是 a ring of light around a religious drawing or painting,例如 Artists usually put *halos* around the heads of saints, angels and Jesus Christ,用在這裡再合適不過了。

》例文五

劍橋的鐘聲為她響起

張達明

原文：

1997 年**鄧亞萍退役**，以英語專業本科生身分進入清華大學學習。第一堂課英語老師問她："你的英語水平是什麼程度？"鄧亞萍囁嚅道："我能寫出 26 個英文字母。"在費了九牛二虎之力後，總算寫出了有些是大寫、有些是小寫的 26 個字母，她不好意思地對老師說："我現在只有這個水平，不過**請老師放心，我一定會努力**，也會趕上其他同學的！"

在當天的日記中她寫道："我現在是清華大學最差的學生，但我相信，**過不了多久我就會成為清華最優秀的學生。**"

但對於只上過小學二年級的鄧亞萍來說要想成為一名合格的大學生談何容易？讀書的清苦和孤獨，雖然不同於球場的訓練，但面對**天書般的英文單詞**，她需要付出比別人多幾倍的辛勞。以至於到後來，**每天清晨起床，她都會發現枕頭上有大把大把脫落的頭髮。在打球時，她兩眼視力都是 1.5，畢業時一只眼睛的視力已下降為 0.6 了。**

後來，鄧亞萍不但以優異的成績獲得清華大學英語學士學位，而且獲得了英國諾丁漢大學碩士學位。一次，鄧亞萍回清華看望英語老師，老師建議她去劍橋讀博士。

於是，鄧亞萍**拿著清華老師的推薦信**，迫不及待地拜見了劍橋大學校長艾莉森‧理查德，把讀博士的想法和盤托出。理查德對她說："**劍橋只收最聰明的學生。雖然你是世界頂尖級人物，但學術背景一定要過硬…… 如果能讓薩馬蘭奇給你寫封推薦信，那當然再好不過。**"鄧亞萍覺得，讓薩馬蘭奇寫封信不算什麼難事，但令她意外的是，薩馬蘭奇並**不支持她上劍橋**，對她說："你已經有了兩個學位，應該馬上**回國效力**，而不是讀什麼劍橋博士。"

她誠懇地對薩馬蘭奇說："請您放心，即使我讀完了劍橋博士，也絕對要回到我的祖國去，我上劍橋，是希望以後能更好地為我的祖國效力。"薩馬蘭奇被鄧亞萍的**誠懇和決心**所打動，為她寫了推薦信。

在劍橋，鄧亞萍拿出打球時**不服輸**的勁頭玩命地學習，把研究方向定位於"2008 年奧運會對當代中國的影響"。**2004 年春節假期，她為了趕寫論文，放棄了與親人團聚的機會。**朋友們勸她："即使讀學位，也不必和自己較真，找個'槍手'

— 171 —

代筆寫論文不也能過關嗎?"但她說:"我讀博士絕不是為了'鍍金',我既然上了劍橋,就絕不會投機取巧走捷徑,更不會弄虛作假! 我盼望著那一刻,當我帶上劍橋博士帽時,劍橋大學城里所有教堂的鐘聲都為我響起來!"

2008 年 11 月 29 日,當劍橋大學校長理查德在學校禮堂前的草坪上親自授予鄧亞萍經濟學博士學位,並為她戴上劍橋博士帽時,劍橋大學城內所有教堂的鐘聲頓時響起來。那一刻,她淚流滿面,哽咽著說:"在經歷了 11 年的艱辛後,今天我終於圓了劍橋博士的夢,激動的心情絕不亞於奪得奧運會金牌。"

——《讀者》,2009(17)

譯文一

The Cambridge Bells Ring for Her

Deng Yaping was accepted as a student by Qinghua University after retirement as a world-class *table tennis athlete* in 1997. In her first class, the English teacher asked her: "How much do you know English?" "Well, I can write the 26 letters of the alphabet." She answered haltingly. With tremendous effort, she wrote out the letters, without the distinction of capital and small forms. She said embarrassingly: "This is all I can do with English, but you can *rest assured* that I'll work hard and catch up with the others."

In her diary on that day, she wrote: "Now I'm the worst student in the university, but I'm sure *I'll be the best soon.*"

It was no easy job for a person with only *elementary education of grade two* to become a qualified college student! She had to endure different kinds of hardship, loneliness and *absence of ordinary comforts* from the life of an athlete. The English textbooks seemed to be as illegible as *books from heaven* to her. She had to make efforts many times more than others in her study. Because she was over-hardworking, *she kept losing hair and suffered from serious nearsightedness.*

After years of arduous work, Deng Yaping not only completed her Bachelor study with excellent achievement but also got her Master Degree from Nottingham University of England. She didn't stop her study here. At the suggestion of her teacher of Qinghua University, she was determined to obtain a PhD in Cambridge University.

With her teacher's recommendation, she eagerly went to Cambridge University and paid a visit to the president, Mr. Allison Richard, who said to her: "Cambridge only takes the most intelligent students. You're a *first-rate* figure in the world, but your academic research capability should be truly proficient if you want to be a student in this university. However, if you can get a recommendation from Mr. Samaranch, *we'll consider your application.*"

Deng Yaping thought there wouldn't be a problem in getting that, but to her surprise, *Mr. Samaranch didn't support her plan*, saying that what she should do now was *to render her service to her country* rather than to get a PhD.

Deng Yaping said earnestly to Mr. Samaranch: "My intention to study for a PhD is to serve my country better. I will go back to China as soon as I finish my study." Moved by her *honesty and determination*, Mr. Samaranch *wrote the recommendation for her.*

With the same tenacious and dauntless spirit as she had when playing table tennis, Deng Yaping devoted herself heart and soul to her study. Her research orientation was "The effect of the 2008 Olympics on modern China." During the Spring Festival in 2004, she was too busy working on her dissertation to be reunited with her family. Some of her friends said to her: "A successful person like you doesn't have to take the study so seriously. You can find a '*helper*' to write the paper for you."

Deng Yaping said with a severe countenance: "My purpose of studying for a PhD is *not to acquire a gilded reputation, or to gain advantage by trickery, certainly not to resort to deception either*, but to enhance my abilities. I'm looking for the moment when I'm put on the PhD mortarboard by virtue of my own effort, all the Cambridge bells will ring for me."

That day came at last. On November 29th 2008, when President Richard conferred the doctorate to her, she was all in tears. *Choking back sobs*, she said: "Having worked hard for eleven years, I've realized my long-cherished dream to be conferred the doctorate from Cambridge. My excitement at the moment is no weaker than getting a gold medal in the Olympics."

譯文二

The Cambridge Bells Ring for Her

Deng Yaping was accepted by Tsinghua University after she retired as a world-class *table tennis player* in 1997. In her first class, the English teacher asked her: "How much English have you learned?" "Well," she answered haltingly, "I can write the twenty-six letters of the alphabet." With tremendous effort, she wrote out the alphabet, but with no distinction between capital and small letters. "This is all the English I know," she said in embarrassment. "But ***believe me***, I'll work hard and catch up with the others."

That day she wrote in her diary: "Now I'm the worst student at the university, but ***I'm sure I'll be the best, and soon.***"

It was no easy job for a person with only a two-year elementary education to become a qualified college student. She had to endure all kinds of hardship and loneliness, ***a life quite different from the one she had been used to in the years of her training for the sport. The English textbooks were total strangers to her.*** To study them she had to work many times as hard as her peers, so hard that before long she would find locks of hair ***on her pillows every morning when she got up, and her eye-sight dropped from*** 1.5 ***on the visual chart before she retired to only*** 0.6.

However, after years of arduous work, Deng Yaping won her bachelor's degree with honors at Tsinghua, and a master's degree from Nottingham University of England. She didn't stop. She planned, at the suggestion of her English teacher at Tsinghua, to study for a PhD at Cambridge University.

Once she made up her mind and ***armed with*** a letter of recommendation from her teacher at Tsinghua, she paid a visit to the president of Cambridge.

"Cambridge is for the most intelligent students," the president told Deng. "You're a ***world-class celebrity, but you need a matching academic background to make the grade.*** However, if you can get a letter of recommendation from Mr. Samaranch, we may consider your application."

Deng Yaping never thought that getting Mr. Samaranch to do that would be a problem. But to her surprise, ***Mr. Samaranch thought otherwise.*** He said to her that with two college degrees, the first thing she should do was ***to get a job immediately and work for her country***, not get a PhD.

Deng Yaping insisted on her request. "With a PhD I will be able to serve my country even better," she said. "I will go back to China as soon as I finish my study at Cambridge." Moved by her ***motivation***, Mr. Samaranch complied.

At Cambridge, Deng Yaping gave full display of her dauntless, ***win-every-game-at-all-cost spirit*** of a table tennis player that she once was, when she worked on her PhD thesis on the effect of the 2008 Olympics on modern China. The writing of the paper kept her so busy in 2004 that she had to stay in Britain during ***the Spring Festival, a traditional holiday in China for family reunion.*** "No need to work this hard," one of her friends commented, "even when it's a thesis paper; you can get a *ghostwriter* to do it. " Deng Yaping refused. "I'm not doing this to adorn my résumé," she said. "*I don't believe in shortcuts*; *I believe in honest work.* I'm working my way towards the day when I put on my PhD mortarboard with all the bells in Cambridge ringing for me. "

That day was November 29, 2008. On that day Deng, *her face awash with tears of joy*, was conferred the doctorate of economics to the ringing of the bells in Cambridge. *With tears sparkling in her eyes*, she said, "Today is the day for which I've been working for as long as eleven years, the day when my dream would come true. I'm as much exited as when I won my Olympic gold medals. "

【分析】這篇文章介紹了鄧亞萍傳奇經歷中最感人的片段,充分體現了一位世界級運動員、奧運會冠軍成名之後繼續不屈不撓,努力奮鬥的精神,讀來異常感人。但是,如何才能恰如其分地譯好這篇短文,讓外國讀者了解鄧亞萍,還是要費些思量。

1) **鄧亞萍退役**——原文開頭沒有介紹鄧亞萍的身分,因為對中文讀者來說沒有這個必要,但譯文必須點明。譯文一譯作 world-class table tennis athlete,其中有誤,athlete 是指田徑運動員,因此譯文二改譯為 table tennis player。

2) **過不了多久我就會成為清華最優秀的學生。**——譯文一是 I'm sure I'll be the best soon,非常平淡,譯文二改譯為 I'm sure I'll be the best, *and* soon。雖然只加了一個逗號和 and,但是此句的力度完全不同了,這樣翻譯更能體現鄧亞萍的決心和信心。

3) **請老師放心,我一定會努力**——"放心"一詞含義很多,可指"別著急","信任"等,譯文要根據上下文而定,例如:

· 他做這事大家都很**放心**。Everyone *trusts* him to do the job.

· 他對大夫的醫術是一百個**放心**。He has *full confidence* in the doctor's skills.

· 這個人總不讓人**放心**。This man is *not reliable* at all.

這個詞在此處的意思是"請老師相信我",英語是 believe me,譯文一譯成 rest assured 意思是"請別著急",顯然與原文不符。

4) **天書般的英文單詞**——"天書"是漢語中常用的比喻,意指"看不懂的書或文字"。譯文一直譯為 as illegible as *books from heaven*,意思可以是"神聖"或"上帝所賜",並沒有"看不懂"的意思。譯文二的譯法正確:The English textbooks were total strangers to her。

5) **每天清晨起床,她都會發現枕頭上有大把大把脫落的頭髮。在打球時,她兩眼視力都是1.5,畢業時一只眼睛的視力已下降為0.6了。**——譯文一把本來很生動的描述給簡化了：Because she was over-hardworking, she kept losing hair and suffered from serious nearsightedness，雖然也算通順，但趨於平淡。譯文二譯成…before long she would find locks of hair on her pillows every morning when she got up, and her eye-sight dropped from 1.5 on the visual chart before she retired to only 0.6，保持了原文描述的生動和具體的特點。

6）**拿著清華老師的推薦信**──這里的"拿著"是"為了某件事做好準備"的意思。譯文一用了 With her teacher's recommendation，雖然不能算錯，但也是平淡無味。譯文二譯為 ***armed with*** a letter of recommendation，可以說是傳神之筆，armed with 是比喻用法，意思是鄧亞萍把"清華老師的推薦信"看作敲門磚，來申請劍橋大學。

7）**"劍橋只收最聰明的學生。雖然你是世界頂尖級人物，但學術背景一定要過硬…… 如果能讓薩馬蘭奇給你寫封推薦信，那當然再好不過。"**──這段話是回譯，即最初的原文是英語，譯成漢語後再回譯成英語。但是，要想還原英語原文是不大可能的。譯文二的翻譯是相當到位的。尤其是"世界頂尖級人"──world-class celebrity，"學術背景一定要過硬"── matching academic background to make the grade，"那當然再好不過"──we may consider your application，譯得自然貼切。

8）**不支持她上劍橋**──這是典型的中國式表達法，其實，薩馬蘭奇只是想法不同罷了，沒有支持不支持一說，所以此句不能像譯文一那樣直譯，譯文二的改譯是正確的：Mr. Samaranch thought otherwise。

9）**回國效力**──譯文一譯成 to render her service to her country，過於正式，不像人們平時的說話方式，譯文二所譯更為合適：to get a job immediately and work for her country。

10）**誠懇和決心**──譯文一是 honesty and determination，雖然這是直譯，但與原文不符，因為鄧亞萍說"With a PhD I will be able to serve my country even better"就是表達了她讀博的 motivation，譯文二的譯法正確。

11）**不服輸**──譯文一 tenacious and dauntless spirit 不如譯文二譯得生動，因為 her dauntless, win-every-game-at-all-cost spirit 更像一個世界冠軍的精神風採。

12）**2004 年春節假期，她為了趕寫論文，放棄了與親人團聚的機會。**──春節時與親人團聚在中國是盡人皆知的傳統習俗，但英語讀者不見得知道，所以必須說明 the Spring Festival, a traditional holiday in China for family reunion，否則鄧亞萍刻苦攻讀的精神表達得不夠充分。

13）**找個"槍手"代筆寫論文**──"槍手"在漢語中帶有貶義，譯文二用了一個中性詞 ghostwriter，去掉了那層貶義，譯得合適。

14）**絕不會投機取巧走捷徑，更不會弄虛作假！**──請一個 ghostwriter 代筆是西方國家常有的事,所以不存在 to acquire a gilded reputation, or to gain advantage by trickery,更沒有 to resort to deception 的意思,譯文一的譯法太過,譯文二譯成 I don't believe in shortcuts; I believe in honest work 正好與上文的 ghostwriter 相呼應。

15)**她淚流滿面,哽咽著說**——譯文一翻成 Choking back sobs,純屬誤譯,因為這個短語的意思是 to try hard to prevent your feelings from showing,但是,當時鄧亞萍流的是"激動的淚水",不必"強忍",譯文二的譯法 With tears sparkling in her eyes,譯得充分。

通過以上對這五個譯例的分析,我們應該認識到翻譯不可能是一蹴而就的事,翻譯從初稿到終稿,不知要經過多少次推敲潤色才能達到令人滿意的程度。對於這一點,尤金・奈達說得好:

One of the most surprising paradoxes of translating is that there is never a completely perfect or timeless translation. Both language and culture are always in the process of change. Furthermore, language is an open system with overlapping meanings and fuzzy boundaries—the bane of logicians but the delight of poets. (Nida, 1993:5)

這應了國人常說的那句話:"沒有最好,只有更好。"這種永遠追求"更上一層樓"的精神對於一個翻譯來說是必不可少的品質。這種品質只有在對兩種語言不間斷的對比分析和持之以恒的翻譯實踐中才能獲得。

思考題

1. 對譯文的潤色和審讀要遵循什麼原則?
2. 有人認為審讀要分為兩種方式:一是對照原文,仔細審查,看內容是否忠實於原文;二是撇開原文,只讀譯文,看譯文是否流暢、自然。你贊成哪種方式?

國家圖書館出版品預行編目(CIP)資料

漢英翻譯基礎與策略 / 李孚聲 著. -- 第一版.
-- 臺北市 : 崧燁文化, 2019.01

　面 ；　公分

ISBN 978-957-681-777-9(平裝)

1.英語 2.翻譯

805.1　107023864

書　　名：漢英翻譯基礎與策略

作　　者：李孚聲 著

發行人：黃振庭

出版者：崧燁文化事業有限公司

發行者：崧燁文化事業有限公司

E-mail：sonbookservice@gmail.com

粉絲頁　　　　　　　網　址：

地　　址：台北市中正區重慶南路一段六十一號八樓 815 室

8F.-815, No.61, Sec. 1, Chongqing S. Rd., Zhongzheng
Dist., Taipei City 100, Taiwan (R.O.C.)

電　　話：(02)2370-3310　傳　真：(02) 2370-3210

總經銷：紅螞蟻圖書有限公司

地　　址：台北市內湖區舊宗路二段 121 巷 19 號

電　　話：02-2795-3656　　傳真：02-2795-4100　　網址：

印　　刷：京峯彩色印刷有限公司（京峰數位）

定價：350 元

發行日期：2019 年 01 月第一版

◎ 本書以POD印製發行